Consequences

For All Her Poor Choices

Shelly L. Foster

To my big bro Ron & my big sis Dot —
I love you more than you'll ever
know. Thank you for loving me.
All my love, Shell 4-10-05

Royal Peacock Publications

P.O. Box 931

Dayton, NJ 08810-0931

www.Royal-Peacock-Publications.com

Published by:

Royal Peacock Publications

P.O. Box 931

Dayton, NJ 08810-0931

www.Royal-Peacock-Publications.com

rppbooks@sbcglobal.net

Copyright @ 2004 Shelly L. Foster

First Printing – March 2005

Printed in the United States

ISBN: 0-9764930-3-9

Edited by: Hope Thompson

Cover Design by: Royal Peacock Publications

ACKNOWLEDGMENTS

Giving all the honor and glory to my Heavenly Father, who guides and directs my path.

Thank you to all my family, friends and readership who have embraced my work. I truly appreciate your encouragement and excitement.

Thanks to all who have contributed to my writing efforts and creative energy. I am blessed to have people like you in my life!

Prelude

As you may recall from part one of this saga, Cynthia

was sucked in by Thomas Alexander, a former schoolmate who had a hand in the murder of her husband, Jordan; a business acquaintance, Mary and another friend, James. Cynthia's daughter Chris was also raped by Thomas, unbeknownst to either of them until they moved in with him and Chris recognized a tattoo on his chest.

His accomplice was Cynthia's Uncle Bobby. Once Cynthia and the police were on their heels, they fled the country, and weren't punished for the murders.

Cynthia and Chris have spent the past few months piecing their lives back together, but out of the blue, their lives get turned upside down once again, in the blink of an eye.

How will they handle things this time?

CHAPTER ONE

1

"**R**un! Run! Cynthia, run!" Ardelia grabbed Cynthia by the

arm, pulling her along the downtown streets of Chicago in fear for their lives. They ducked into the doorway of a closed restaurant. They stood holding each other, shivering with fear. Moments later, they heard footsteps coming in their direction. They were paralyzed by the mere thought that they were in danger. As the rapid footsteps got closer, their embrace became more intense. They squeezed their eyes shut, accepting that they would die in each other's arms. The footsteps stopped at the doorway, which made their adrenaline race, their hearts pound and their anticipation of death a reality in their minds. As they waited for their demise, a calm, soothing voice asked, "Are you okay?"

They were overwhelmed with relief and within a few seconds they opened their eyes and released their embrace, but they were unable to speak right away. After collecting themselves, Cynthia spoke first. "We were being followed by two men, so we hid in this doorway."

Ardelia chimed in, "We thought you were them, and we just knew we were about to die."

One of the men reached into his pocket, pulling out a police shield to identify who they were. The other one offered to take them home. They declined, but asked to be escorted to their car.

Once at the car, they hopped into Ardelia's Mercedes and peeled out fast, leaving the officers standing at the curb in their smoke. The two men glanced at each other then proceeded to their car.

Ardelia and Cynthia went straight to Cynthia's house, arriving in record time. They went inside and flopped down on the sofa, still amazed by their ordeal.

Cynthia had thought her life was getting back to normal. After Thomas and Uncle Bobby disappeared, she figured moving on would be fairly easy to do. For a while, normalcy was a thing of the past. For months Cynthia had fought her way through an emotional battlefield, giving all she had to Chris and her business. Chris was finally able to sleep alone and in her own room again. Cynthia had her business relationships gripped in the palm of her hand. A sense of security and a road to recovery was in reach. Now this... *Who could that have been following us?* Cynthia thought. Her mind was on overload, ready to explode at any moment. She realized what was happening and took control. There was no way she was going to allow Thomas to reek havoc on their lives again.

While Cynthia and Ardelia sat in silence collecting their thoughts, the doorbell rang. They both jumped up from the sofa and crept to the door. After the ordeal they'd just experienced, neither was too eager to open the door. Ardelia peeked out of the bottom corner of the window, but was only able to see one set of feet, a large pair of penny loafers with no indication who they belonged to. Cynthia cracked the door enough to get a full frontal view and was relieved to see it was only Frank. Frank had a questioning look on his face as he observed Cynthia's hesitation to open the door. Once over the threshold, he questioned what was wrong.

Cynthia and Ardelia each gave an account of their perilous day. Frank's demeanor was a bit alarming. He didn't seem to be surprised by their story. Cynthia immediately noticed how unconcerned he appeared to be so she commented, "What's up with you Frank? You don't seem to be the least bit concerned."

"No, that's not it at all. I'm just taking it all in. I thought this mess was in the past and I didn't expect to hear what you just told me. Do you think the men you saw were Thomas and Uncle Bobby?"

"We don't know who they were. By the time they were close enough to see their faces, we were too busy running away." Cynthia responded.

Ardelia interjected by adding, "At the time, we didn't care who it was. We knew we were in danger, and acted accordingly. What difference does it make who it was? Our lives were threatened and the bottom line is we escaped unscathed."

"It matters if it was a random situation or if it's Thomas and Uncle Bobby. You should be prepared to deal with whatever fall out may come later. Either way, you're still scared and panicked so..."

Ardelia cut him off in mid sentence, "Of course we are still scared, but you act as though we shouldn't have any emotions."
"I just think that if it's an isolated situation, and Thomas and Uncle Bobby aren't in the picture, there's nothing to fear."

Cynthia raised a brow, irritated by his blasé attitude. It was apparent that his company was no longer welcome, so Cynthia stood and walked to the door.

"Thanks for stopping by, Frank." she announced as she opened the front door.

Frank rose from his seat, leaving without saying a word. Cynthia slammed the door as he exited, and returned to the den with Ardelia.

"Can you believe how nonchalant he was?"

Ardelia shook her head and drifted into her own thoughts. Frank's statements made her replay the events, searching for more detail in her mind. She figured if she thought about it more methodically, she would recall something that her emotions had allowed her to omit. Ardelia laid her head back onto the back of the sofa, propped her feet on the coffee table and closed her eyes. Cynthia moved to the recliner and curled up in a fetal position. Shortly, they were both asleep.

Meanwhile, Frank was next door at his place, feeling sorry for himself. He had always been weak for Cynthia, but she'd been humiliating him ever since he was mistakenly arrested for the murders and he'd suggested that Chris might be involved. At any rate, he was not riding on her bandwagon anymore. He only stuck as close to her as he did to help get the stink of the murders off his back. Actually, he'd begun to loathe her. In his eyes, Cynthia was wicked and needed to be brought down a peg or two. He pondered his thoughts for a while then turned his attention to a movie. Eventually, he was snoring on the sofa.

Several hours passed and Cynthia and Ardelia were stirring about the house. Cynthia decided to fix them something to eat, so she went to the kitchen to prepare a meal. Ardelia joined her in the kitchen striking up a light conversation. Neither of them wanted to think about what had happened earlier, no less talk about it. Before long they were laughing about the outfit Cynthia's secretary Marge had worn to the office.

"The fashion police wouldn't have written her a ticket they would have taken her ass straight to jail in that get-up."
Ardelia was laughing hysterically when Cynthia made the comment, but managed to get her own dig in as well.

"They would have stripped her, burned her clothes then took

her to jail butt naked. Those clothes didn't deserve a ride to the police station."

"Do you think I should make her get a makeover? Maybe I could give her a bonus, strictly for shopping purposes."

"Hell, she would spend the whole wad on a closet full of floral, striped and polka dot mistakes. You need to send her to a fashion consultant, and go with her."

"I don't want to be seen with her at all. Even with twenty-first century clothes, she still reeks of Ben-Gay."

"And don't forget, the stockings that fall and drape over her shoes."

Cynthia covered her mouth with her hand, gasping, and on the verge of tears. She waved her other hand in the air, in an attempt to stop Ardelia from commenting, but it didn't work. Ardelia came back with more.

"What about the wig? Don't forget the mangy wig that smells like old cooking oil."

Choking and sniffling, Cynthia bent over, holding her side, and ran out of the kitchen. Ardelia ran behind her, laughing and joking more about Marge. Cynthia ran into the bathroom, locking Ardelia on the other side. Ardelia was pounding on the door and shouting jokes at the same time.

"Maybe if she took a bath more often than once a week on Saturday nights, her odor might not linger and the stench wouldn't hit you in the face before you enter your office!"

Cynthia jerked the bathroom door open, with eyes as big a golf balls.

"Girl, are you telling me you can smell her when you enter my office?!!"

"You can't smell it? I never said anything 'cause I thought you knew."

"I must have become used to it. Oh my God, my clients smell that stinky odor when they come in my office!"

"Yep, I would imagine so. I smell it every time I come to see you."

Cynthia went back into the kitchen and Ardelia followed. Cynthia sat at the kitchen table, placing her head in her hand. Ardelia could tell Cynthia was embarrassed, so she let up on teasing her. Cynthia raised her head and the embarrassment showed all over her face. She wasn't embarrassed by Ardelia smelling the odor, but she was definitely embarrassed if her clients could smell Marge's stench.

"I had a client come see me today that I was a little taken with, and he was interested in me as well. I hope he doesn't think I'm the stinky one. Maybe that's why he got the hell out of my office so fast."

"Anyone that comes in your office knows it's Marge that's stinking. The smell leaves your nostrils three feet into your office. He knows it's not you, so don't sweat it."

"That's easy for you to say. You're not the one who people think smell like a sour pickle closed up in a jar for a long period of time."

Ardelia pointed at Cynthia and shook her head. They both fell out laughing again.

"That was wrong. She doesn't smell that bad."

"The hell she doesn't. She is F U N K Y. I'm going to have building services come down and fumigate tomorrow. Then I'm going to have a heart to heart with ole' girl about her personal hygiene. And then...she simply must go to a fashion consultant. Her nineteen sixty-nine wardrobe can no longer be worn at my place of business."

Cynthia was irritated with the thought of her clients having to smell that terrible odor when coming into her office.

"Let's not spend anymore time talking about stinky old Marge. Let me tell you about this guy I met today."

"I don't want to burst your bubble, but the last thing you need is to get involved with anyone right now."

"Why not? It's been months since all that mess with Thomas. Am I expected to be a hermit?"

"No, you're not expected to be a hermit, but I would think that with all you went through, you wouldn't want to be bothered. I thought you were going to focus on your daughter and your work?"

"Well, Ms. Smart Ass, we talked about a business venture.

He's good looking, but that's not the focus of the relationship."

"I'm sorry, but you didn't say it was for work."

"You didn't give me a chance to say much of anything before you lit into me. It's not about work with the firm. It's a new business venture for me to consider."

"What kind of business?"

"Real estate investments."

"How will you be able to juggle your current business, your child and real estate investments?"

"There won't be much leg work. I will only be investing as a silent partner."

A concerned look swept across Ardelia's face, but she didn't speak her mind. She knew if she spoke, Cynthia wouldn't like what she had to say, so she said nothing.

"What? What is it, Ardelia?" Silence filled the room, but Ardelia wouldn't say a word.

"Come on, spit it out, Ardelia."

"I'm sure you don't want to hear what I have to say."

"Yes, I do. Tell me."

"I don't think you should get involved with anyone you don't know, especially investing your money. Why would you take a chance with your money with a stranger?"

"There are five investors to purchase a mall that is drowning. We're going to revitalize the mall, and the community. There's not a lot of risk."

"Not a lot of risk? Not a lot of risk? Giving your money to someone you don't know is a risk, Cynthia."

"I feel good about it, and it's going to make me a lot of money."

"How did you come to know this guy? What made him ask you in on the deal?"

"We met a few weeks ago by chance, while I was having lunch. We talked for hours then we scheduled time to meet."

"So, like I said, you don't know him."

"Right, Ardelia. I don't really know him, but I think I'm going to invest anyway. What's the worst thing that could happen? I could loose a few thousand dollars, but I stand to gain several million. The higher the risk, the higher the reward."

"Whatever, I'll be right here when you need a shoulder to cry on."

"Why are you putting your pessimism into my space? I can do without your negative energy."

Ardelia pushed away from the table, grabbed her purse and car keys, and left.

All the way home, she thought of nothing, but how Cynthia was making a big mistake. She didn't understand how Cynthia could be so careless and trusting, after all she'd been through. Part of her wanted to turn her car around and go back and shake some sense into her, but she knew Cynthia would only dig her heals in if she felt pressured to change her mind. She felt a pang in her gut that said Cynthia was headed for trouble. Nonetheless, she was hopeful things would work out as Cynthia believed they would.

Back at Cynthia's house, Cynthia was loafing around, unable to eat. She kicked up her feet, stretching out on the sofa to relax. Although she believed in her friend, and valued her opinion, she had never gone to Ardelia about business decisions before and her decisions had always worked out fine. She was ready to make more money and the investment required minimal dollars up front. She didn't feel any amount of apprehension, so she decided to go with her instincts. She picked up the phone and called Anthony D'Amato to set up a time for them to finalize their deal. They agreed on Friday at three o'clock. After finishing their conversation, Cynthia wrapped herself up in a blanket and drifted off to sleep.

CHAPTER TWO

2

The next day was pretty hectic for Cynthia, but after

finding a break in her schedule, she spent about an hour having a heart-to-heart talk with Marge. Marge didn't receive the coaching as well as Cynthia would have liked, but she agreed to see the fashion consultant and work on better, personal hygiene, just the same. She left Cynthia's office almost in tears. Upon her exit, she ran into the guys coming to fumigate the office. The mere sight of them made Marge's blood boil. As the crew entered Cynthia's office, their faces twisted as the funky smell nearly knocked them off their feet. Even though they didn't dare comment, their expressions told it all. Cynthia asked if she needed to leave while they took care of their business. She was instructed to leave for at least two hours. She figured with that much time on her hands, she may as well leave for the day. She packed her briefcase and headed for home.

On the way home Cynthia had an incredible urge to have a drink. She drove to a nearby, quaint, jazz spot, that she used to frequent many years ago. She strolled in, exuding her usual confidence and a slightly snooty air. She was confident enough to be misconstrued as arrogant and just snooty enough to be a hair shy of a snob. Whenever alone, this demeanor was her shield of protection. This way was most comfortable for her to keep the average 'Joe' from considering her easy prey. She sat at the bar, crossed her legs and ordered her drink.

There were about five men standing in a corner at the opposite end of the bar, winking, smiling and flirting with her. She did her best to ignore the old geezers, but they still believed in their 'pipe smokin', hair so grey it's yellow, polyester jumpsuit wearing' minds, that they were still good catches. She smiled as she sipped on her drink, all the while thinking, *His stomach is where his chest used to be and the bell on his pant legs could ring louder than the church bell on Christmas morning. And you, 'Mr. false teeth that move up and down whenever you talk' should just not wear them at all if you can't keep them still.*

Before she could have a thought about the other two, she envisioned him laughing and his teeth hitting the floor. That thought caused her to choke on her drink. Mr. Bellbottoms took a few steps to come to her aid, but she waved him off, indicating she didn't need help.

Damn, this used to be the spot. Maybe this is the hangout for geriatrics now. I don't see a soul in here my age. I wish... As she turned her barstool in a different direction, the sight made her forget the ending to her thought. A Pale grey Armani suit, white shirt, pale pink with grey pinstriped tie and Feragamo shoes was worn by a man who looked like he's just been peeled off of a billboard. His hair was groomed to perfection, facial hair trimmed to enhance his strong bone structure, and he smelled like he just stepped out of the shower. Flawless was the only word to describe how captivating he was. Cynthia's mouth dropped open, and she damn near started drooling. Her mind knew that she needed to get a grip, but her body was slow to respond. As he slowly glided his way past her, he nodded. Her confidence was being held captive by the image of perfection that had just graced her presence. He took a seat at a table, alone. Within moments, the waitress was at his beck and call. By the time his drink was served, he was joined by two other men. One of them ordered his drink and approached Cynthia at the bar. Once she focused, she realized it was her new real estate partner, or partner to be, Tony. He invited her to join them at their table, which she gladly and graciously accepted.

Cynthia slid down from the barstool and followed Tony to the table. He introduced her to "Mr. Flawless", Savonte' Black that is, and Evan Roberts. No matter how cool she tried to be, Savonte's presence made her forget her own name. After talking with them for a while, her nerves began to settle, and she found it quite easy to interact with Savonte'. Regardless of the flawless, confident image he carried, he was warm, humble and funny; not intimidating at all. Once they all relaxed for a bit, Tony mentioned the 'business' word and it was shop talk for about an hour or two. They were so engrossed with the potential of their investment they hadn't realized how late it had gotten. Tony leaned over to Cynthia and said, "There's no need for us to wait until Friday to finalize our partnership. Not only have we discussed every detail that we would have Friday, but you've met the other investors as well. Well, actually, there's one more, but he is truly a silent partner. You will probably never meet him."

Cynthia scanned their faces as they patiently awaited her response. She briefly hesitated, then responded by saying, "It all sounds perfect. I'm sure this is going to be the investment of a lifetime, but before I make a firm commitment, I have to sleep on it. I can let you know by Friday."

After giving her spiel without taking a breath, she exhaled. Tony and Evan nodded, while Savonte' winked, and gave her a half cocked smile. His pearly, white teeth glistened through the small crack in his lips, making her yearn to suck his face like you would a juicy, sweet, California orange. Little did she know they were on the same page.

As they each exchanged business cards, Savonte' softly stroked her palm with his index finger. She knew what that meant and was more than happy to oblige. Their sly communication was like watching a silent movie, anticipating the next move. Although she was a little smitten with Tony at first, Savonte' had blown him right out of the water.

Each of the men stood as she rose from the table to leave. The senior citizens were still standing in the corner by the bar. They stood erect, or as erect as they could, repositioning the polyester, wiping the drool oozing from the corners of their mouths, and cheesing like Cheshire cats. Since Tony had made mention during their conversation that they met there regularly, she knew she'd see the seniors again. *It couldn't do any harm to be nice to the old goats. I may need them one day,* she thought. She raised her arm chest level and wiggled her fingers, bidding them a cute little farewell. That little gesture did them a world of good. They stuck out their chests, actually, their stomachs and smiled, showing all thirty-two of their perfectly made, unsecured, floppy teeth.

After Cynthia made her exit, she took her time walking to her car. Her cell phone rang as soon as she sat down inside the car.

"This is Cynthia," she answered.

"This is Savonte'. I'm walking out of the club. Where are you?"

"I'm sitting here in my car, about a half block down." She peered out of her rearview mirror and saw him standing on the sidewalk.

"I can see you. Turn to your right and walk down the block. I'm in a BMW convertible."

They held the phone without any conversation until he reached the car. He leaned in the window and asked if he could follow her home. She nodded and suggested she drive him to his car.

She was anxious to see what he was driving, anyway. *Hmmm, wouldn't you know his vehicle makes a powerful statement, too . . . a Jaguar.*

He got out of her car and into his. Minutes later they were on their way to Cynthia's place.

Once inside, Savonte' relaxed on the sofa, while Cynthia fixed drinks. She knew good and well that she'd already reached her alcohol threshold, in fact she was drunk, but she was home and wanted to loosen up a little more. She was graceful and dainty and still able to have an intelligent conversation. Even though talking was the last thing she wanted to do, she listened, as he told her how much money she stood to gain by partnering with them. After a while, she didn't hear a word he was saying. She had zeroed in on his succulent lips, which he licked occasionally while he talked, and was aching to kiss him.

If he says more than ten more words, I'm going to cover his mouth with mine and suck the juices collecting in the corners of his mouth.

At the close of the last syllable of his tenth word, Cynthia moved in for the kill. He saw it coming and decided to have some foreplay. Just as she was close enough to feel his breath on her face, he reached up and lightly stroked her hair. He took the time to place the hair on the right side of her face behind her right ear, and did the same to the left side. He then cradled her head and gently brought her face close to his. She still hadn't gotten any lip action and he knew she was longing to taste him. He kissed her ear, and down her neck, until he couldn't take it anymore. She allowed him to lead her down whatever path he chose. She willingly followed, without leaving breadcrumbs to find her way back. Step by step, they made their way to the bedroom. She removed his clothes piece by piece, taking the time to hang each one, as he stood before her raw and lean. If he were a steak, she'd be licking the plate by now. She gave a lovingly firm push to his chest, pushing him onto the bed. He lay there posing, while she took as much time undressing herself as she took undressing him. She kept her cool, but her desire was building, her anticipation was intoxicating and her vagina was a volcanic sea of hot lava.

Before she could make her way over to the bed, he was on his feet coaxing her to join him. If they both weren't trying so hard to keep their ultra deluxe, calm, cool images, they could probably have had some fun. Cynthia realized it and dropped her guard. Once she gave in, she was given the 'Royal Lady' treatment, instead of the 'I'm going to hold back as long as she's as strong as me' attitude.

He took extra special care of every intricate part of her body. He wasn't in a hurry, but he didn't make her wait. He took her to a place where ecstasy was a one bedroom flat and she was being served in the penthouse.

Hours had passed, and she didn't want him to leave. She usually wasn't needy, but she wanted to play the damsel in distress. It was hard to determine if he would fall for the damsel in distress routine, so she played it close to the vest and didn't say a word. When she got up to shower, he was sound asleep. She ran hot water in a pale, got two wash cloths, a loofa sponge and shower gel. She washed him up and powdered him down. She rolled him to one side of the bed, slid off the soiled sheets then slipped the clean ones on each corner. She rolled him onto the clean half of the bed, pulled off the soiled, and fit the clean sheet on the other half of the bed. She sprinkled more powder and covered him with the clean sheet and blanket. She took time to shower and joined him in the bed.

The night became a thing of the past, as the sun graced the window. As it turned out, she didn't have to be a damsel in distress after all. He was next to her when she opened her eyes. She leaned over and asked if he wanted breakfast. He responded by nodding his head while he stretched, but was pulling her close in the process. Apparently, the breakfast he had a taste for wasn't bacon and eggs. She slid into the cuff of his arms, taking a mental ride back to the penthouse, while he captivated her mind and her body. He took his time pleasuring her and fulfilling her needs.

After a tune-up and a jump start, she was ready for whatever the day would bring. She was hoping he would stick around for maintenance every now and then, if for no other reason. They showered, dressed and went their separate ways.

Savonte' was mesmerized by their spontaneity, placing him in a mental fog while driving home. Cynthia cruised to the office, utterly amazed by the connection she'd made with him. She floated into her office, oblivious to the world around her. Marge spoke as she passed her desk, but Cynthia didn't hear her. She did notice that Marge didn't reek of Ben-Gay, and the funk didn't slap her in the face as she entered her office. She dropped her purse and briefcase on her desk and eased into her chair. She laid her head back on the chair, slipping into a state of euphoria. She stayed there for fifteen minutes or so, before returning from her journey.

She had been in la-la land since she first laid eyes on Savonte', and really didn't want to deal with reality. However, reality was being crammed down her throat, as she remembered that she had an appointment. Marge entered to inform Cynthia that her client had arrived. She had Marge get coffee and detain her appointment for ten minutes so that she could get prepared. She scurried about in an effort to transform herself into the professional her client was expecting to meet with. She was truly not in a frame of mind to discuss business, but it paid the bills. She greeted her client in the reception area and showed her into her office. Jacqueline Fitzgerald was her name. She owned a chain of fitness centers throughout the Chicago area. Her clientele had grown beyond the capacity of the current building designs. She wanted the new and improved models to be on the cutting edge in order to handle future growth. Her plan was to design and build three new developments that were energy efficient. All sides would be glass to provide solar energy.

Their meeting went so well, Ms. Fitzgerald signed contracts before she left. Cynthia walked Ms. Fitzgerald to the elevator, sucking up to Jacqueline, and not having a problem doing so. Cynthia gave Marge the contracts to get the other partners' signatures, make copies, send one to Ms. Fitzgerald's office and file. She placed a call to get the process team on board and then mentally calculated the expected dollar amount she'd personally make on the deal.

As the cash machine rang in her head, Cynthia was comfortable investing in the real estate deal. She called Tony D'Amato's office to give him her final decision. She got his voice mail and left him a message to call her. She thought it odd that whenever she called him, she could never reach him live. She always had to leave a message and await a call back. She shrugged it off and didn't give it a lot of thought. The last thing she needed was to be paranoid about everyone she met.

The rest of the day was fairly mild. Phone calls and paperwork consumed her afternoon, keeping her from her Savonte' fix. She was able to stay focused until she'd signed the last document in the pile. Five-thirty had rolled around and the office was like a ghost town. Her partners usually stayed late, but their offices were locked up tight. Stinky Marge had left, and didn't bother to say goodnight.

Cynthia gathered her things and headed for home.

CHAPTER THREE

3

Cynthia's house was a lonely place since Chris was on

vacation with Lolly and her family. Cynthia showered and moped around in her robe. Halfway through a really boring movie, nervous energy was swirling through her veins. She jumped up from the sofa, went to her bedroom, squirted on a soft, sensual cologne, put on a short, multi-colored pastel chiffon dress, and yellow, suede sandals that tied around her ankle. She combed her hair in an up-do, securing it with a rhinestone clip.

Once in the car, she lowered all the windows to take in the fresh air as she drove. With lust on her mind, she pointed her car in the direction of Syncopations, the jazz lounge where she'd met Savonte'.

The other day when she met Savonte', the club had a dull, dry crowd, but this night there wasn't a parking space in sight. She circled the block, and luckily someone was pulling out directly across the street from the club. As she crossed the street, a cool breeze whisked through the chiffon, cooling down the moisture on her skin. She leisurely made her way past the crowd that had gathered near the front door.

She was hopeful that Savonte' would be in the mix, but tried not to solely depend on his presence to have a good time. She found an unoccupied seat at the bar and carefully stepped up on the wrung of the stool and took a seat.

Drinks started coming out of nowhere. She asked the bartender who was being so kind, but he wouldn't say. As the fourth drink was placed before her, there was a tap on her shoulder. Low and behold, there stood Savonte'. Her stomach tied up in knots of excitement, her palms started to sweat and words formed, but nothing would come out. She acknowledged him with a wink, while sipping her drink. It was a pitiful attempt to appear in control, but that's all she could muster up. He lightly stroked her cheek with the backside of his index finger, causing her to smile.

They talked for a bit until she needed to go to the ladies room. The fire in Savonte's eyes burned as he noticed her chiffon dress sway with every move. She was commando under the layers of chiffon and her provocation made his nature rise. The mere thought that she was gutsy enough to come out that way sent his libido through the roof.

When Cynthia returned, Savonte' was in a hurry to get her out of there.

"There are too many people in here," he said, as he threw his head back towards the door.

"Would you like to..."

Before he could finish his sentence, she interrupted.

"Yes!"

She started laughing and covered her face with her hands. She couldn't believe she'd shown how anxious she was, but she wanted him and didn't give a shit how it came across. He walked a few steps behind her as they left, watching her chiffon dress sway back and forth. The movement of her hips was so inviting, they were calling his name.

Savonte' was parked around the corner in an eight-level, covered parking lot, so she drove him, yet again, to his car. The upper levels were blocked to incoming cars, which caused them to park on the first level and take the elevator up to the seventh level, where his car was parked. On the way up, Savonte' got a whiff of Cynthia's perfume and reacted without giving it a second thought. He cornered her in the elevator, raising her dress to her waist. She was panting, her mouth watered and she broke out into a cold sweat. Fortunately, no one tried to take the elevator while they rode up and down several times. Once when it stopped, the doors opened, but no one was there, or at least, no one got on. They were so into each other, they didn't have a clue what was going on around them.

Savonte' polished her off, as she gripped the guardrails tight enough to swell the blood vessels in her hands. Once her feet touched the floor, the chiffon fell into place, he zipped his pants and they exited the elevator.

They got into his car, but neither said a word until they were going down the ramp to the third level. He looked over at her and smiled. She burst into laughter, holding her face in her hands and stomping her feet on the floorboards. Her laugh was very unique and the sound of it made everyone who heard her laugh as well. Savonte' got a kick out of her and it took him completely by surprise that she was able to make him laugh like that. He was serious and sophisticated, and usually didn't break that mode. Deep down he was regretting he'd ever met her. He hadn't had a Jones for anyone in years and she had entered his dreams, making him fiend for her like a junky. She didn't know he was as hooked on her as she was on him, but she knew she had it bad. She exited his car and instead of continuing their night together, they went their separate ways.

Cynthia found herself pulling into Ardelia's driveway. It was late, but she let her friend in anyway. Cynthia had a mischievous grin on her face as she walked into the house. She knew Ardelia was curious, so she toyed with her a little before giving her the scoop. While Cynthia went on and on about her escapades, Ardelia waited to comment. As soon as Cynthia finished, Ardelia gave her a piece of her mind.

"Cynthia, what in the world are you doing?"

"What?"

"Why are you going down this path again?"

"Going down what path?"

"Having sexual relations with people you barely know… that path."

"Is there a play book that gives a specific amount of time before you sleep with someone?"

"No, and that's not the point and you know it."

"So, tell me. What *is* the point?"

"Your behavior is very unbecoming and I'm afraid that you could be setting yourself up for heartache, but more importantly, danger."

They sat back on the sofa and stared at each other for a few moments. Ardelia then restated her position.

"You are making a big mistake, Cynthia. I think you should stop this out of control train from rolling. If you don't, you're going to crash."

"Why can't I have fun without your nagging? This is just fun. Don't make it more than that."

"Because your fun could become disastrous, and guess who stands to get hurt the most? Chris, that's who."

"Chris? How'd she get in the mix?"

Ardelia took her fist and knocked on Cynthia's forehead.

"How'd she get in the mix? What the fuck is wrong with you?"

"Nothing," Cynthia replied.

"This conversation is going nowhere. I don't care to discuss it any longer. When this relationship spins out of control, just let

Chris come stay with me. Don't drag her into your bullshit again."

After making that statement, Ardelia got up and stormed out of the room. Cynthia sat for a few minutes, and then left the house without a word. On the drove home, Cynthia was fuming. She couldn't remember ever being that angry with Ardelia, but Ardelia had crossed a very fine line.

Once in her house and snuggled in the bed, Cynthia replayed the conversation with Ardelia, trying to see Ardelia's point of view, but she couldn't see past her own wants and needs. She was so blinded by Savonte' that Chris didn't seem to be her priority anymore. It was a good thing Chris was on vacation with her friend, or she'd be upset with Cynthia's behavior, too. She lay there tossing and turning for a good while before drifting off to sleep.

Ardelia on the other hand, couldn't sit still, much less sleep. She was having major trouble with Cynthia's oblivion. There was no way in hell a woman as sharp and on the ball as Cynthia, couldn't see the impact Savonte' would have on her life.

She should have learned enough from the Thomas fiasco, to make her gun shy for any man. Why would she let someone she doesn't know dominate her? I know she's a sex fiend, but damn, the bamboo can't be that good.

Her thoughts eventually gave her a break, so she turned her attention to a silly comedy on television.

The wee hours of the morning had crept in and Ardelia still hadn't been able to sleep. She could clearly see the downward spiral that was more than likely to rip Cynthia's life apart, and wondered if it would be even more devastating than before. But her biggest concern was how to keep Chris from being affected by it all.

CHAPTER FOUR

4

Ring, ring, ring.

"Yes, hello," Evan answered in an irritated tone.

"Evan, this is Savonte'. Did I catch you at a bad time?"

"Lately it's always a bad time. This latest investment project is consuming me man."

"I would help you out, but international tax law is your baby. You usually handle that without breaking a sweat."

"Yeah, but I'm setting up the new Swiss account we talked about."

"I still don't see that as a problem for you, you da' man."

"The problems will come if I don't set up the tax haven and the funds don't transfer exactly right. We don't need anything or anyone traced back to us."

"You're right. Especially now, with five of us to account for, I see your point. Why don't we meet at Syncopations tomorrow and discuss where we are with this?"

"That'll work. How's about six-thirty?"

"Six-thirty works for me. I'll call D'Amato and tell him."

"Cool."

Savonte' immediately called Tony to let him know about the meeting, but conveniently forgot to inform Cynthia.

The day seemed to drag on and on with no end in sight, but evening finally came. Cynthia had just stuck her key in the lock when she heard the phone ringing. She was able to grab it before it went to voice mail. On the other end, a deep sexy voice said, "Hello, Cynthia." Her forehead wrinkled, as she tried to put a name to the voice in her mind. She'd never spoken to him on the phone before, but she got the same goose pimples she did when they were together.

"This is Savonte'."

Her eyes lit up and her heart fluttered with excitement.

"Hey Savonte', what made you call?"

"I was wondering if you wanted to grab a bite to eat with me."

"Sure, but I just walked in the door so I'll need time to shower and change."

"That's fine. I figured about seven-thirty. May I come pick you up?"

"That'll be great."

Once they'd hung up, she dashed up the steps, stumbling over her feet to perfect herself before he arrived.

She stood in the closet pondering over what to wear. She

couldn't quite decide whether to wear a suit or a sexy dress. Even though at the end of the night she expected to bed him, she kind of wanted the professional look.

There it is. This is perfect.

At twenty-five past seven, the doorbell rang. She had just slipped on her shoes and was ready to go. When she opened the door, Savonte' smiled as he took a step back to admire how nice she looked. Pink was the color that enhanced her complexion, her eyes and her hair color. The pink dress contoured her curves, while the jacket added a little swing. The pink, pointed toe mules and the silver jewelry completed the look.

Savonte' complimented her as he stepped inside. They both felt like school kids, as they stood in the foyer with nothing to say. The silence was uncomfortable for them both so Cynthia offered to fix drinks before they left. She knew the alcohol would loosen them up, but was hoping not too much. He was one of the most sought after eligible men in town and she really wanted to dine and be seen about town with him. Savonte's drink was gone in a few gulps, while Cynthia took little sips of hers. Although she hadn't finished her drink, she asked, "Are you ready to go?"

"After you," he replied.

The moment they entered the restaurant, all eyes were on them. Actually, Savonte' drew the crowd. He was so fine, he almost didn't look real. He was a breathtakingly gorgeous work of art, which made Cynthia feel as if she just added brush strokes of color to an already perfect painting. Nonetheless, she was okay with whatever stroke she could provide.

As they were led to their table, the heads turned, the eyes rolled and the whispers started.

You bitches can whisper, stare or whatever the hell you feel like, but he's mine, for tonight anyway...ugly bitch, fat bitch, smart bitch, retarded bitch...all you bitches can kiss my ass, Cynthia thought as the stares burned her skin. She was hoping that the ugly thoughts floating around in her head didn't show on her face. She smiled and flirted with Savonte' across the table, while a table of four women kept their eyes glued to them.

Since you bitches are watching us, like you're at the damn AMC theater, why don't I give you something to see? Cynthia thought with venom.

Using both feet, she maneuvered her feet free of her shoes. Since she and Savonte' were seated in a booth, it gave just enough privacy, but lent enough visibility to let the onlookers see. She eased down in her seat, rested her buttocks on the edge of the seat to allow her barely five-foot legs to reach across to his seat. Once she was completely comfortable with her balance, she touched his ankle with her nicely pedicured toes then moved her foot slowly up his leg, until her foot rested in his crotch. All the while, she gazed into his eyes, and he into hers. As she took a sip of the drink that had just been brought, she glanced from the corner of her eye, to her audience. She'd gotten to them alright. Savonte' got into the groove and played along. He taught her a lesson or two about playing footsy though. He got so into her foot play, his eyes glazed over. She had no idea he had a foot fetish in the worst way, until he abruptly dismissed the waiter when he tried to take their order. She sat back, propped one arm on the back of her seat, and ran her fingers through her hair, while he got off playing with her feet. He worked the pressure points in her feet enough to make her moist. When his breathing became short and his eyes started to roll, she knew she needed to get the freaky Jeannie back in the bottle. Before he started to moan or grunt, she slowly pulled her foot from the cradle of his crotch. He was gone...far, far off in his own zone. He didn't realize she'd removed her foot. He didn't know where he was, or probably what day of the week it was, at that moment. Cynthia whispered his name a couple of times, in an effort to reach him in the far off place he was visiting.

Her soothing voice was able to connect to whatever state he was in and gently brought him back to reality. Not long after his return, he situated himself and they burst into laughter. They were giggling so much Cynthia hadn't noticed the four women had left the restaurant.

Savonte' motioned for the waiter to return to the table. As they ordered, the waiter was a tad perturbed that he was dismissed earlier. Savonte' gave him a stern 'don't fuck with me or I'll give you a penny tip' look, that clearly put the situation in perspective for Mr. Waiter. He left them to converse, while he placed their order with the chef.

They had some light-hearted, small talk, without any mention of the business venture. Savonte' was hoping she wouldn't bring up business, for fear she'd learn about the meeting with the partners. She wasn't invited, 'cause in their narrow minded beliefs, they didn't think she would fully understand the international workings of their joint venture. She was good enough to invest her money, but not considered smart enough to be included in the fundamentals of how her money was made. They probably really knew how sharp she was, and were fearful that she'd become a threat to them.

Cynthia wasn't the least bit interested in discussing business anyway. She was thrilled to be with him and took advantage of her time alone with him. Their food arrived at the table, but Cynthia was having a hard time getting it down. She didn't understand the nervousness that had tightened her stomach, when she had already fucked the man ten ways from Sunday. Savonte' wasn't having any issues. He was inhaling his steak and shrimp like it was his last meal.

After dinner they had an after dinner cocktail, then headed for the car. They slowly cruised around the city, laughing and talking, while the cool, night breeze blew peaceful, serene air throughout the car. They cruised by an all night tattoo parlor and Savonte' convinced Cynthia to go in with him. Inside the parlor stood a big, burly, six foot three inch grizzly with tattoos all over his body. Cynthia scrunched up her nose, the corners of her mouth turned downward and she slapped Savonte' on the arm.

"Why did you drag me in here?"

"I had an urge to get another tattoo and thought we both could get one."

"Did you fall out of a tree and bump your head?"

Cynthia turned to leave, but Savonte' smooth talked her right back to his side. Big Grizzly asked if they wanted to look at the book of selections. Savonte' nodded and Grizzly handed him the book. When Savonte' opened the book and moved it in front of Cynthia, she drew her arms up close to her chest tucking her fingers into a fist.

"I'm not touching that book . . . no telling what's on it. It looks greasy and grimy."

Savonte' started laughing, as he browsed the book. He found one that he thought would be great for her, and then he found one for himself. Grizzly showed them to the booth and Savonte' agreed to go first. Cynthia watched closely, as Savonte' got pricked with the needle and squirted with the ink.

"Girl, lighten up. It doesn't hurt at all."

"My skin is more delicate than yours. I don't think I can do it."

"Yes, you can. Just loosen up while he works on me, then I'll keep you loose while he works on you."

Cynthia rolled her eyes and blew air from her mouth while Grizzly finished Savonte'.

Once finished, Grizzly nodded for Cynthia to move into position. Cynthia looked over to Savonte' and asked, "Where should I put it?"

"Take off your jacket and lay down on your stomach."

He scooted her dress up to her waist, pushing his index finger onto her left butt cheek. She wore a thong, so there was no need to remove her undergarments.

"Right here on this cheek. That's where I want it."

"What color?" Grizzly asked.

"Black . . . a deep, dark, velvety black."

Cynthia raised a brow and turned to look at her behind.

"I don't want a big, black glob of ink on my behind."

"Relax. It'll be nice. Wait until you see the finished product."

"By then, it'll be too late to do anything about it!"

"It'll be fine. Chill out, woman."

Grizzly looked at Savonte' for the go ahead, and then started to work. Cynthia jumped, squirmed and clutched Savonte's hand throughout the entire ordeal.

Why the hell did I let him talk me into this bullshit? I'm getting a damn permanent mark on my body, listening to some fly by night asshole that probably won't be in my life very long. I should have my ass kicked. I should kick it myself," Cynthia thought.

She turned her head away from Savonte' and faced the wall. She lay there impatiently, pissed with herself and wanting desperately for the ordeal to be over. She heard the sound of the gun cut off, then a light touch to her butt cheek. Savonte' was tracing the tattoo with his index finger, while gently massaging her butt cheek. Although she'd been anxious for it to be completed, she didn't jump up to see it. She lay there in silence, wondering what her behind must look like and if the ink would stain her dress when she pulled it down. They stayed for a bit to allow the ink to dry. Cynthia stayed on the table while Savonte' went to the front to pay. When he returned, he helped her off of the table and they went to the car.

When they finally arrived at Cynthia's, Savonte' walked her to the door. Since he'd left the keys in the ignition, she didn't bother trying to get him to stay. She was still on full from the last two times they were together, plus she was upset that she had gotten that damn tattoo. He gave her a quick peck on the cheek and left.

On his way home, he thought of nothing but her. His quick exit was prompted primarily by her attitude. She was cold and bitter on the drive home, plus he was really taken by her and wanted to withdraw. She didn't realize it, but she had him hooked. The sad thing was that he was only hooked on the sex. Her sex appeal and provocative behavior aroused him like no one else had. Without the sex, he could care less about her. He'd survived in his business dealings because he was ruthless and shrewd. If she got in the way or slowed down the plans for their new real estate deal, he'd trample all over her. The other two, Evan and Tony, weren't quite as wicked, but they always managed to float to the top. Cynthia was approached about the deal because she was well known from her partnership with the Robinson, Cavil and Lee architectural firm. Plus, she was targeted for her financial contributions and that's all the participation they expected her to have. As long as she let them run the business and she sat back to get paid, there wouldn't be any problems. Some of their dealings are underhanded tactics that she won't be privy to. They were high rollin', well dressed, mild mannered shysters. It would be in Cynthia's best interest to get laid every now and then and not get too close.

Cynthia lay in bed longing to be with Savonte', but realizing he didn't want to be bothered tonight. Just as she began to drift off to sleep the phone rang.

"Hello?" She answered.

"Hey, Sugar," Savonte' spoke from the other end of the phone. Cynthia perked right up and sat up in the bed to talk to him.

"Where are you?"

"Home," he responded in a sorrowful tone.

"Is something wrong?"

"Nope. I just wanted to hear your voice and thank you for joining me for dinner."

"It was my pleasure. Why'd you rush off?"

"I was a little tired and wanted to go to bed."

"You could have done that here."

"Oh sure, but how much sleep would we have gotten?"

He was not about to admit that he was trying to wean himself from her. His ego wouldn't dare allow him to reveal that he was weak for her.

"I wouldn't have bothered you."

"Maybe not, but the smell of your sweetness next to me would probably have made me bother you," he said in a playful tone.

"Okay...if you say so."

She knew it was necessary for her to keep her cool. They talked for a few minutes longer, and then hung up.

I was almost asleep before he called. Now I have Savonte' on the brain and I'll never get to sleep, she thought.

She flipped through the television channels, searching for something to take her mind off of him, but nothing quite did the trick. She folded her arms across her chest and lay on her back, staring at the ceiling. Eventually, she managed to drift off.

CHAPTER FIVE

5

Morning came quickly and was ticking away, before

Cynthia awakened. It was a damn good thing she didn't have any appointments, since it was after eight a.m. Once she was out of the bed, she moseyed along getting dressed. Sleeping so late was completely out of character for her, but she figured *what the hell?* She was a partner and she didn't have to punch a time clock. She was financially stable and about to make even more money with the real estate investment.

She arrived at her office shortly before eleven. Marge had the nerve to give her a disapproving look as she approached her office. She breezed past Marge without any acknowledgment. *How dare she look at me that way, the stinky old crab.* Cynthia opened her blinds and started preparing for the day while Marge stewed at her desk.

Cynthia was just about to buzz Marge to bring her coffee when Marge came through the door. Even though Marge was old, stinky and occasionally wore her stockings draped over her shoes, she was very efficient. Her maturity allowed her to put her personal feelings aside and deal with business as a professional should. She sucked up her emotions and placed the coffee tray on the credenza near the window. Cynthia reluctantly said 'Thanks' as Marge turned to leave. Marge left without responding.

As she read through some documents, the senior partner, Maurice, came into her office. It was rare for Maurice to visit her without an agenda. Although his demeanor didn't show it, he had to have something serious to discuss. He stayed for better than thirty minutes without a hint of trouble or concern. *Hmmm, I guess I was wrong . . . guess he just wanted to bond.* After Maurice finished his cup of coffee, he returned to his big, lavish, corner office, so Cynthia went back to reviewing paperwork. She hated dealing with all the paperwork that followed the customer meetings and dinners, the negotiations and contracts, but without the paperwork, no one would get paid. As she was finishing up one set of documents, Paulie and Billie, the other partners, came in to invite her to lunch.

What is up with all the bonding today? We never do lunch, Cynthia said to herself.

Cynthia snapped her head back in shock that they'd asked her to join them. The inquisitive look in her eyes said it, but it had to come out.

"What's going on that you want me to join you for lunch?" Paulie spoke right up. "We realized that we don't include you very much, so we thought we'd reach out to you today."

*Not true. You really didn't want to ask me to come back, but
you know that I can bring in the business. Now with the fitness center
deal, you know that you're going to get paid in a big way. You can't
bullshit me, but I'll play,* Cynthia thought intently before responding.
She smiled, then replied, "Sure, I'll go."

Billie was such a control freak, she had to drive. They went
to a seafood restaurant that had the best luncheon buffet. For three
women, they put a big dent in the buffet. To their surprise, they
found themselves having an enjoyable time. Cynthia was the live
wire on the team. The other partners were stuffy, way too polished,
overly sophisticated and just plain ole' boring. They didn't have
much of a sense of humor and they took everything seriously.
Cynthia often wondered how either of them produced children. She
couldn't imagine them having sex at all, but maybe their spouses were
the lively ones, or maybe they weren't as boring in the bedroom as
they were in the office. She had them in stitches telling them about
Marge. They were laughing as they walked back to the car.

"What a delightful afternoon," Billie offered.

"Yes, it was. Thanks for inviting me."

Paulie turned to the backseat where Cynthia sat and said,
"We must do this more often."

Cynthia stared blankly out the window as they drove past
Syncopations. The sight of the place took her to 'Savonte'ville'.

"Cynthia? Where did you drift off to?" Paulie asked.

Cynthia's thoughts had shifted into overdrive as she thought of her times with Savonte'. Naturally she wouldn't tell Billie or Paulie anything about him, but she sure wanted to. Getting through the night without him was difficult, but she'd seemingly managed through the day, at least until she saw the club. Slowly, she mentally twisted and turned her way back down the path to reality.

"Cynthia! Did you hear me?" Paulie asked once again, as she snapped her fingers in Cynthia's face. Cynthia blinked a couple of times, and then responded, "Sorry, I have a lot on my mind. What did you say?"

"Hell, I don't remember now."

Billie snickered, knowing that Paulie was pissed that Cynthia wouldn't share her thoughts. Paulie was quite the nosey one. She knew everything about everybody, everywhere, and couldn't stand for anyone to hold back information. Paulie turned and faced forward, noticeably hot under the collar. Cynthia sat back, folding her arms, itching to give the skinny on her fun times with Savonte', but determined not to draw them into her personal space. They drove in silence the rest of the way back to the office.

Cynthia's phone rang the moment she sat at her desk. The client on the other end of the phone was the last person she wanted to speak with. Catherine Garrett owned several strip malls, and was as exciting as watching a caterpillar go through its metamorphosis. Every time they'd met, Catherine bored Cynthia to tears. She was so boring, Cynthia didn't care if she got her business or not. But surprisingly, Catherine suggested they meet and have a drink at

Syncopations. Well, that suggestion definitely sparked Cynthia's interest. She raised an eyebrow and stared at the telephone receiver.

"Sure, I'd love to meet you there."

"Great, can you make it by six?"

"Not a problem. I'll be there."

The instant Cynthia hung up the phone, she scrambled to put the finishing touches on some of her paperwork. She was thrilled to have an excuse to go to Syncopations. The thought of running into Savonte' really got her juices flowing. By five-twenty, she was on her way out the door. She took her time getting there, although she was reeling with anticipation. She arrived about five minutes 'til six, but Catherine hadn't arrived yet. The usual geriatrics were leaning in their favorite spot near the bar. She acknowledged them as she passed. She took a seat at a table in the back where she could see anyone who stepped through the front door. The light from the outside and the dim lighting around her table prevented her from being seen very well. After her drink was delivered to the table, Catherine came through the door. She met her halfway and showed her to the table. As Cynthia turned to sit, she found Catherine talking to the geriatrics in the corner.

Hmmm, wouldn't you know it. She knows the stale old goats. Hell, she's got on a polyester suit that damn near matches the one the guy standing next to her is wearing. They could easily pass as the Bobsey Twins." Cynthia thought as she smiled.

Cynthia sipped her drink, while Catherine enjoyed the company of the guys at the bar. Over the top of her glass, Cynthia caught a glimpse of Savonte', Evan and Tony coming through the front door. Even though she knew they hung out there, a gnawing feeling knotted tightly in her stomach. She sat back in her chair to observe them. She was hoping they wouldn't notice her until she was ready for them to know she was there. Catherine seemed to be in heaven and Cynthia was glad she wasn't at the table distracting her. Cynthia's focus was on her new partners and why they were meeting without her.

Granted, this meeting may be just pure pleasure, but something tells me they're up to something they don't want me to know about, Cynthia reminded herself.

Cynthia watched closely and waited for Savonte', Evan and Tony to show some sort of sign that their meeting was more than coincidence. Shortly before her next drink arrived, Evan reached into his briefcase, pulling out three folders. He placed one in front of himself, then handed one each to Savonte' and Tony. The discussed the papers for quite some time. Before they could finish and put the papers away, Cynthia was standing over Savonte's shoulder. Evan and Tony looked like they'd seen a ghost. Their mouths dropped open, their eyes grew wide and beads of sweat popped out on their foreheads. Although their reaction announced guilt, Savonte' played it cool. He turned to her, expressing joy to see her, "Hey gorgeous, have a seat." As Cynthia was shifting the chair, Savonte' slid the folders into his briefcase. He immediately engaged in conversation to steer her away from asking any questions. It worked for a little while, and then Catherine approached the table. Cynthia initiated introductions around the table as Catherine took a seat. Something during the introductions didn't feel right to Cynthia. She got the distinct impression that they all knew each other, but no one let on. She observed, while they all chatted, before launching her inquisition.

"So, what were you all studying when I walked up? Was it something to do with the investment that I should know about?"

"Well, uh..." Evan stammered.

"Hey what's going on here? Why the questions and accusations? What would make you think we would keep you in the dark about this investment?" Savonte' interjected. But before Cynthia could respond, Savonte' pounced again, "As much money as you've sunk into this investment you are definitely part of this team. We value you a great deal."

What a load of horseshit. He must really think I'm green. I can feel in my gut that something's not right, but I'll let him think I'm buying it.

"I guess I must have misread you all. I think I've dealt with so many people who have screwed over me, that there's a huge block when it comes to trust. Forgive me for my paranoia."

Everyone at the table was tight with tension, but the moment Cynthia completed her sentence, everyone relaxed. Their shoulders slumped and their sighs of relief could have blown out a dozen candles.

Cynthia knew they were waiting with baited breath to see if she'd explode, so she handled the situation with grace and style. She knew it best to keep her suspicions to herself. They'd gone to an extreme to keep something from her for a reason. The only way to learn the reason was to keep her mouth shut and her eyes open. What was puzzling was the role that Catherine played. Her invitation to Syncopations at the same time the guys were meeting was more than a coincidence. Bonding with Catherine on a regular basis was on Cynthia's list of things to do. Tolerating Catherine's boring ass and being seen with the polyester queen would be the hardest part, but somehow she had to get to the bottom of whatever was going on.

No one could figure out the best way to end the evening without appearing guilty, so they continued to converse and drink. After several hours and many, many drinks later, they were all toasted. Cynthia was hoping one of the drunks would speak a sober mind, but not a chance. Catherine was very chatty, but she hadn't said anything incriminating. The alcohol had made Cynthia tired and sleepy, so she decided to be the first to make an exit. Catherine followed suit and suggested they walk to their cars together.

Once the door closed behind them, the guys buried their heads in their hands.

"That was too fucking close. From now on, if we have a covert meeting it should not be in a public place," Savonte' commanded.

"Hell, what were the odds that Cynthia would be here at the

same time?" Evan belted.

"The odds were better for her, since ole' Savonte' here is banging her. Who knows how often she comes here, hoping and expecting to run into him," D'Amato retorted.

Savonte' gave him an intense glare, but didn't respond. He figured if he lit into him, it would only put a strain on their partnership. There was too much at stake to jeopardize it all for a piece of ass. They had one more round of drinks before hitting the road.

CHAPTER SIX

6

Cynthia made it home and curled up in the bed to

watch television. Something said by one of the characters in the
movie caused her to think about Catherine. The evening spent with
Catherine forced Cynthia to recognize Catherine's wickedness.

*This wicked, sneaky bitch is up to something. But we don't have
anything in common outside of our business relationship to make her
want to do me any harm. Her polyester suits and sensible shoes set
us worlds apart. There's no way we have any interest or people in
our lives in common. Hmmm, but what's up with the vibe I got? She
knows Anthony, Evan or Savonte', I'm sure of it, maybe even all
three. Could she be the silent partner they told me I'd probably never
see? Nah, they referenced a man, not a woman. My instincts are
flashing red lights for a reason. I can't ignore it, but I can't drive
myself nuts without any evidence to prove she's foul. This is going to
take more than just asking a few questions, but how do I trap her?
Fuck it, I'm not going to lose any sleep over this bullshit,"* Cynthia

thought.

Cynthia went back to watching the movie when the doorbell rang. She glanced at the clock, glowing eleven-forty eight p.m. She jumped up and flung her robe over her shoulders. Mumbling and cursing all the way to the door, she yelled, "Who is it?"

The voice on the other side of the door was muffled, although it was definitely a man's. She stepped over to the window and peeped out of the corner of the drapes. She couldn't believe her eyes. It was Maurice. She hurriedly opened the door asking, "Maurice! What in the world would bring you to my house at this hour?"

Maurice shook his head as he stepped inside.

"I am very disturbed and we need to talk."

Cynthia showed him to her living room, and offered him a seat. She sat on the edge of her chair, as she anticipated what Maurice had to say. He had a look of disgust and Cynthia was certain this visit wasn't to bond.

"Cynthia..." Maurice stopped, dropped his head, and wrung his hands. When he raised his head, he had flames in his eyes. This made Cynthia nervous and uncomfortable. The suspense was killing her.

"What Maurice? What could be disturbing you?"

"I am furious with what I've learned." A lump arose in his throat and once again, he was unable to speak. Cynthia prodded and urged him to continue, but he was still speechless. Suddenly, he blurted out; "I have found an accounting error in our books to the tune of hundreds of thousands of dollars!"

"Okay, I can understand the concern, but is it really necessary to discuss it at this hour?"

"I've been struggling with this all day. When I came to your office, that's what I wanted to discuss."

"Why didn't you say something then?"

"I decided to dig a little deeper and get more details first."

"And what did you find to make you drive to my house in the middle of the night?"

"That's what's so difficult. My findings indicate the error leads to you."

"Me? How? What?"

"Several commissions paid out to you, and all a minimum of one hundred thousand dollars over and above what should have been paid out."

"There has to be a logical explanation. I don't know what it is, but we have to get to the bottom of it. I don't have that kind of money in my accounts."
Maurice shot her a loathsome glare.

"What's that look for?"

"I had accounting pull the direct deposit information on you and all the money has been posted into your accounts."

"That couldn't be. I just checked my bank accounts the other day. I don't have anywhere near the amount you're suggesting."

Maurice reached into his jacket pocket and pulled out a white envelope. He stretched his arm and slapped the envelope into the palm of Cynthia's hand. She opened the envelope, finding a bank statement in her name. Her mouth fell open over what she was seeing.

"I never opened this account! I don't even bank at this bank, Maurice!"

Maurice's nostrils flared as he then mumbled; "Oh sure."
"Oh sure? Oh sure? You have the gall to sit in my home and accuse me of embezzlement? Maurice, I'd like for you to leave."

Maurice stood and headed for the door. Cynthia paced closely behind him, fuming . *Asshole. Someone has set me up and you think I have so little integrity that I would steal from the company that feeds me? If you weren't the senior partner of the firm, I'd tell you what I really think; you big water-head, stuffy old bastard,"* she thought with a vengeance.

As Maurice stepped out of the house he turned to speak, but as he opened his mouth...Blam! Cynthia slammed and locked the door, turned off the lights and returned to bed.

It was three-eighteen a.m. and Cynthia still hadn't fallen to sleep. She was outraged that Maurice would entertain the idea that she'd embezzled from the firm.

I had lunch with Paulie and Billie, yet they never said a word. Could this be, the reason they asked me to go to lunch with them? Could they be part of this conspiracy or perhaps Catherine? she wondered.

Realizing she wasn't going to get any sleep, she got up and dressed for work. She dressed as if it were eight a.m., instead of four a.m. She wanted to search through as much paperwork as possible. She wanted to believe that she could quickly find the error and bring it to resolution by the time Maurice came in.

She pulled into the parking garage about five-fifteen. Naturally, at that time of the morning, the garage was empty. She turned off the motor, but didn't remove the keys. She placed both hands on the steering wheel, gripping it tightly. Tears came streaming down her face uncontrollably. She began to beat the steering wheel with her fists. *What the hell is happening to my life? How the fuck could things go so wrong, so fast? I'm going to find out who's doing this to me, if it kills me*, she shouted loudly, while patting the tears away with a tissue. She applied more lipstick then headed for her office.

The entire floor was dark, cold and creepy. She felt as though, she'd just stepped inside the screen of a horror movie. She heard rattles, thumps and creeks. She put her high heels into overdrive, and scampered down the hallway, flicking on every light switch in sight. When she made her way into her office, she closed and locked the door. She's been to her office many times late at night and early in the morning, but had never felt uncomfortable or scared. She figured her mind was playing tricks on her, with all the chaos going on around her.

She settled in her chair, pulled files out of the drawer and started reviewing them, word for word, dollar for dollar, to find any discrepancies. After an hour or so, her eyes became heavy, and the need for caffeine overtook her. She was so accustomed to Marge preparing her coffee, she didn't have any idea where the supplies were, or how to use the new machine.

As she placed her hand on the doorknob, she heard footsteps outside her office. She froze with fear, impaired by her own morbid thoughts.

As the person in the outer office turned the doorknob, Cynthia jumped, causing her to knock over a vase of flowers. Naturally, the vase broke and glass shattered. Cynthia took in a deep breath and covered her mouth with her hands. The unknown person tried the knob again, and also gave the door a push. The next thing Cynthia heard were keys. Her eyes stretched open as wide as they could, as perspiration trickled down her face, her armpits and her back. She wanted desperately to bolt and run, but the only place to go was into the arms of the stranger on the other side of the door.

She turned around in circles, taking a step to the left, to the right, backward and forward. She was discombobulated, and unable to make a strategic move. Meanwhile, a key had been placed in the keyhole and the door was beginning to open. Her feet turned into cinder blocks, her legs into rubber and the rippling effects of fear surged throughout her body. With nowhere to hide she put her hands over both eyes as the door slowly opened.

"Cynthia! I thought I heard someone stirring around in here.

I heard something break. Are you okay?"

She knew the voice, although it was the last voice she wanted to hear. She lowered her hands to respond.

"Yeah, I'm fine. I didn't think anyone else was here, and your footsteps and your attempt to get in here, frightened me," she remarked.

"What brings you in so early?"

"How much sleep did you expect me to get after dropping that bomb on me last night, Maurice?"

Still irritated by her slamming the door in his face last night, he didn't bother to respond. He turned and walked out as if she hadn't said anything. Cynthia shrugged her shoulders as she went to make coffee.

While the coffee brewed, she scanned more papers for errors. So far, not one contract had any errors.

Maurice must have conjured up this bullshit in his mind. I can't find a damn thing wrong, with any of my paperwork. I keep copies of all my negotiations, so if he has documents from another source, they have to be falsified.   Cynthia pondered over her thoughts for a few moments, then left to get her coffee. When she returned to her office, she put the coffee cup on the table and flounced onto the sofa. She slowly sipped her coffee, taking in the aroma and the flavor. *Marge's coffee tastes better, but this ain't half bad. It'll have to do until Marge comes in and makes another pot.*

She finished off the first cup and returned to the coffee area to fix another one. As she turned to leave, she bumped into Maurice. They brushed arms as they proceeded in opposite directions. Maurice scratched his head as he watched her walk away.

Cynthia was in no mood to deal with Maurice's attitude or accusations. Once back in her office, she closed and locked the door. She needed more time to dive into the rest of the documents before everyone started coming in. The last thing she needed was for the other partners and the staff to get wind of Maurice's allegations. She wanted desperately to smear Maurice's nose in facts to prove her innocence. At this point, Billie and Paulie probably already knew. If they did, having proof was even more reason to find something . . . anything that could clear her name.

After sifting through mounds of paper and finding nothing to clear her of Maurice's allegations, she thrashed the papers about her desk. She laid her head on her desk and released all the tears that she'd been holding in. After the crying spell, she became enraged. She flung the papers in the air then sent her coffee mug whirling and crashing into the wall.

Apparently, Marge had come into work, heard the crash and tried to get into Cynthia's office. Cynthia heard Marge ask, "Are you okay?" She responded "Yes!" in an irritated tone. She turned her chair to face the window. She simply could not believe that she wasn't able to find any errors in the documents. Wherever Maurice got his information from, it had to have been manufactured. Whoever did it knew enough to make the doctored up documents appear real.

Lately, things had been going fairly well in Cynthia's life and this crisis came from out of nowhere. It was unbelievable how authentic the documents seemed to be. If Cynthia didn't know any better, she would have believed she was guilty, too. She got up from her chair and started picking up the papers strewn all over the floor. Putting them back in order seemed to be therapeutic. She then called maintenance to clean up the coffee and glass. She was not interested in the glares and stares that would come as the day progressed. Knowing that she needed hard proof to make this go away, she got her briefcase and purse, and then headed for the elevator. Luckily, Marge had stepped away from her desk and she didn't have to deal with the likes of her. She patted her foot as she impatiently waited for the elevator. It seemed to be taking forever and the last thing she needed was for the elevator to stop on her floor, full of people she didn't want to face. Unfortunately, when the doors opened, the elevator was packed and everyone was getting off on her floor. She kept her head bowed towards the floor, holding her breath as each person stepped off. No one spoke, so apparently they weren't paying any attention to her. Thinking she was home free, she raised her head before entering. Her eyes met a cold set of eyes glaring at her. As they exchanged places, Cynthia got on and the other person stepped off, all the while never losing eye contact. Cynthia gave her the head to toe once over as the elevator doors came to a close.

Hmmph, guess Maurice has filled the other partners in. Bitch. How dare Paulie look at me with such disgust. I'm innocent, but the partners must have already made it up in their minds that I'm guilty. Now I'm beginning to see that my partnership was no more than a meal ticket. I bring in all the fucking big accounts, while they play golf and go on family vacations. I have busted my ass and they've all benefited, but now I'm treated like I have two fucking heads. Kiss my stretch marked ass, you assholes.

Cynthia got into her car, but just sat there, numb from disbelief. She knew she was the patsy in someone's sick, twisted plot against her. She was convinced that someone was trying to destroy her, but had no clue who it might be. Those who came to mind were part of her past and she hadn't had any contact with any of them in a very long time. More tears flowed, but they were tears of anger. She was no longer going to feel sorry for herself. She knew that she needed the strength to get through this battle. She didn't bother wiping the tears away as she had no indication that they would stop any time soon. She put the car into gear and started on her way.

She really didn't have a destination and simply did not want to go home just to sit and stew over her dilemma. She sure as hell didn't want to go talk to Ardelia. Hearing 'I told you so' was not on her list of options. Chris was due to come home the next day and she wanted to bring this bullshit to a close before her child came home from vacation to another mess. She drove in circles until she got tired of seeing the same scenery. She took off onto the interstate, pushing her BMW to eighty miles an hour. The further she drove, the faster she went. She barreled down the highway, tailgating those driving at a legal rate of speed, pushing them along until they got out of her way. She passed everyone in sight, leaving them in her dust. The tears kept coming and began to blur her vision. She reached up, wiping the tears away, when suddenly...SCREEEECH, BLAM, CRASH, BANG! As she whipped over to pass a slow vehicle, she was side swiped by another speeding vehicle. Both cars jumped the median and toppled onto their sides, skidding across the lanes. The next thing she knew, she heard walkie-talkies, sirens blaring and the sound of a saw cutting through her vinyl, convertible top. She was carefully pulled out of the car and placed onto a stretcher. She couldn't tell who was in the other vehicle or if they were okay. She was quickly rushed to the hospital and into the emergency room. She moved in and out of consciousness while she was being worked on, but she was conscious enough to know that her daughter needed to be cared for once she returned home the next day. She quietly called Chris' name enough times that the nurse asked her who Chris was.

"My daughter." she said softly. "Can you call my friend Ardelia and let her know what has happened? Please tell her to get my daughter when she comes home tomorrow."

"Yes, I will. What is her number?" the nurse asked, as she patted Cynthia's hand.

"It's the first number stored in my cell phone. Does someone have my purse?"

"Yes, it's here under the table. I'll get it and make the call."

Cynthia   then   nodded   back   off.

CHAPTER SEVEN

7

"Hello, is this Ardelia?"

"Yes, who's this?"

"This is nurse King from Memorial Hospital. I was asked to call you by a patient who was just brought in to us."

"Who?"

"Cynthia Evans."

"WHAT! WHAT HAPPENED?"

"She was in a car accident."

"How is she? How badly was she hurt?"

"I can't give you much information, but she's being worked on right now. She wanted you to know and asked that you get her daughter when she arrives home tomorrow."

"Of course I will, but I'm coming over there now."

"Now isn't the time. You won't be able to see her. Why don't you wait a few hours before coming?"

"I'm coming now. I'll just sit and wait. Thanks for calling."

Ardelia changed into a comfortable outfit and stormed out the door. Realizing how fast she was driving, she let up off of the accelerator. The last thing she needed was for she, and Cynthia to be laid up in the hospital. She cruised down the highway, anxious to see about her friend. The further she drove, the longer the road seemed to get. The highway appeared to be endless, with exits further and further apart. She approached a patch on the highway where the traffic slowed nearly to a halt.

As the traffic inched along, she came up on police vehicles and tow trucks. One of the tow trucks was raising a car onto its bed. Every part of the vehicle was scraped and crushed. Ardelia's initial thought was; *No one could have survived that crash*. A few feet ahead, she got a glimpse of Cynthia's BMW. The convertible top was ripped off, the driver's door was caved in and it was lying on its side. The mere sight of the scene brought tears to her eyes. At this point Ardelia was more anxious to get to the hospital than she was before. About three miles down, she made her way down the exit ramp. Three or four blocks later, she turned into the hospital parking lot.

Moving at a rapid pace, Ardelia made her way to the nurse's station. She located nurse King to learn that Cynthia had been taken to a room for recovery. She was sleeping, but nurse King allowed Ardelia to sit in the room with her.

Ardelia sat on the edge of the chair, resting her chin on the guardrail, while holding Cynthia's hand. In less than an hour, Cynthia was coming to. She blinked a few times and could vaguely see Ardelia sitting by her side. She was still groggy and her speech was slurred, but Ardelia was able to make out what she said.

"Is Chris home yet?"

"No, honey, she's not due to come home until tomorrow."

"Oh, I guess I'm pretty messed up, huh?"

Ardelia tried to lighten the moment by attempting to make her laugh.

"I really don't know how messed up you are, 'cause you look like a mummy."

Cynthia attempted to move her arm to feel the bandages, but she wasn't able to move it. Her entire body was racked with pain. Even when she attempted to smile, it hurt.

Ardelia could barely stomach how bad Cynthia looked, but she held back the tears. Moments later, the doctor came in to check on Cynthia. The doctor looked at Ardelia stating, "I'm sorry, but I must ask you to leave while I examine her."

"May I come back in when you're finished?"

"I think it best that she get some rest. Why don't you come back tomorrow?"

Ardelia leaned over the bed rail and kissed Cynthia on the forehead. She told her she'd be back the next day with Chris. She was irritated that the doctor wouldn't let her stay, so she flung her purse over her shoulder and sashayed out of the room.

When Ardelia returned home, she made one of her spare rooms comfy for Chris. She figured she and Chris would need to bring quite a few of Chris' things to her house. From the looks of Cynthia, she was going to need weeks, possibly months to recuperate. With that in mind, Cynthia and Chris would probably need to stay with her for a while.

Ardelia decided to go to Cynthia's house and get some of Chris' things. She figured Chris would have a hard time dealing with Cynthia's accident, and her condition wasn't good. The sight of Cynthia in those bandages would probably scare the hell out of Chris. Contrary to her tough, teenage front, she's fragile and Mommy's little girl. Ardelia was prepared to step in and give Chris whatever she needed to get her through it.

Once she arrived at Cynthia's, she used her key to go in. She gathered up everything she thought Chris would want and need. She knew Chris wouldn't be able to function without all of her teenage paraphernalia and she wanted her to be as comfortable as possible. She unplugged the electronics and carried what she could downstairs. She collected a few things for Cynthia, for when she got out of the hospital.

After taking several loads to the car, she rang Frank's doorbell. There was no doubt in Ardelia's mind that Frank would help her out. He suggested he load the electronics into his truck, then follow her back to her place.

Naturally, Frank was filled with questions. After everything was put into place, he got comfortable on the sofa. Genuinely concerned, he asked, "What happened?"

Ardelia filled him in on as much as she knew and then stood up to leave. Frank got the message that he was no longer needed or wanted, so he stood as well. On their way to the door, he asked,

"How bad is she?"

"The doctor wouldn't tell me much, but she has a broken arm, a broken leg, a cracked rib, a few loose or missing teeth and a slight concussion."

"How much more could be wrong? Shit, that's several months of recuperation time."

Frank shook his head as he stepped onto the porch. Ardelia shut the door without giving Frank a second thought. She proceeded upstairs to Chris' room to put everything in place, and then tucked Cynthia's things into a drawer in the other spare bedroom. After everything was done, she showered and fixed herself a bite to eat.

Now that her tummy was full and she was organized, she relaxed in the bed, flipping through her planner to get the details on Chris' arrival home. She wanted to get there a little early, just in case they arrived sooner than expected. She watched a movie until she drifted off to sleep.

Back at Frank's place, he was sitting on the front stoop, pitching rocks into the yard. He hadn't seen Cynthia for a while, but couldn't bare the thought of seeing her mangled. He got up from the stoop to call the hospital. As he shuffled up the driveway, hands in pocket and head bowed, a car pulled into Cynthia's driveway. Frank stopped, as the Jaguar pulled in. He waited to see who was visiting. When Savonte' stepped out of the car, he spoke to Frank. Frank made his way over to him saying, "She's not home."

"Do you know if she's been gone long or if she'll be back soon?"

"I'm positive she won't be back soon."

"Did she leave town or something?"

"Or something," Frank evasively replied.

Frank was a little reluctant to give up any information without knowing who he was. Savonte' knew he needed to offer Frank something or he wasn't going to tell him a thing. He extended his arm to shake his hand.

"I'm Savonte' Black. Cynthia and I are partners in a real estate investment deal and we've been seeing each other as well. Could you please tell me where she might be?"

"She's in the hospital. She was in a terrible car accident." Savonte' leaned on the car, surprised at what he'd just heard.

"How is she?"

"I haven't seen her, but her best friend told me that she was pretty messed up. I was on my way in to call the hospital when you pulled up."

"What hospital is she in?"

"Memorial."

"Thanks, man."

Savonte' jumped into his car and sped off in the direction of the interstate. The entire drive there, he thought of nothing but how this could impact their investment. He hadn't given her health a second thought. His greatest concern was how she could continue to function as a partner. As long as she could still write a check and make withdrawals from the bank, she could stay in the hospital forever, as far as Savonte' was concerned.

By the time he walked into the hospital, he was dripping with charm and compassion. He got past the nurses' station and into Cynthia's room without anyone stopping him. He stood over her while she slept, finding that her condition looked more serious than he'd imagined. It was quite noticeable that there were several broken bones.

Oh shit, her right arm and leg are broken. That means she won't be able to write or drive for a while. Hmmm, that might work to my advantage. Maybe I'll convince her to let me handle her business for her. She's so damn independent, self sufficient, controlling and stubborn, it'll probably take every ounce of bullshit I know to make that happen," Savonte' thought.

While he stood over her, his chin rested between his thumb and middle finger, with his index finger covering his lips. He was deep in thought, contemplating how best to manipulate Cynthia into giving him control when she opened her eyes.

"Savonte'?" She spoke quietly.

"Yes, honey." he responded, as he moved closer to her bed.

He leaned over and kissed her on the cheek. She immediately started crying and acting as if she were weak, pitiful and needy. Although that was so far from the truth, she could see her world crashing all around her. She was tired of being strong, tired of carrying all the weight, so she took the opportunity to lean on Savonte'. That was his cue that she was vulnerable and the perfect time for him to offer his assistance. She was emotionally drained, mentally exhausted and physically impaired, not to mention that she was drugged from the pain medication.

He brought his face close to hers and spoke softly and empathetically, "Baby, let me help you. Let me worry about paying your bills and handling your business affairs. I'll make sure everything gets done while you recover."

He waited for her response before continuing. She cracked a small smile, let out a sigh of relief, then said, "Thank you. Thanks for caring enough to help."

"To make this easier, why don't I have my attorney friend draw up a document that will legally authorize me to step in on your behalf until you've healed?"

"Okay, but I can't sign the document, so what good will it be?"

"I have a friend at the bank who could possibly come here, and witness and notarize our agreement. It's just that simple. How's that for full service?"

"That's great," she responded, as she drifted off to sleep

again.

Savonte' stood looking down at her with a victorious smirk on his face. He left the room feeling pretty good about himself.

Getting the real estate deal off the ground took a long time. Evan, Tony and Savonte' had so many other deals going on, they needed Cynthia to join the team for a number of reasons. Their silent partner also urged them to get her and made threats if they didn't.

Savonte' called his attorney friend as soon as he got in his car. He was able to catch his friend at the bank just before they closed. He agreed to have the document ready by first thing in the morning. He also agreed to meet him at the hospital in the morning. He then called Evan and Tony and asked them to meet him at Syncopations.

They met up about seven o'clock, where Savonte' gloated about having control of Cynthia's finances. Evan and Tony were both surprised that Cynthia would surrender her independence, less known her money. Savonte' stuck his chest out, boasting that she needed him to handle her business affairs. Cynthia had mentally and emotionally checked out, otherwise she'd never have given him the control.

Actually, she was in a trusting place with him. She really believed that she could trust him to take care of things just as she would have. She was only giving him the authority to write checks for her bills and to invest and deposit money for the real estate investment, or so she thought.

As the second round of drinks were delivered to the table, Catherine walked in with another woman. They headed straight for Savonte', Evan and Tony's table. Savonte' and Tony were stumbling over themselves to offer the ladies a seat. Catherine's girlfriend was stunning. She was tall and thin and wore an awesome platinum haircut. She had one dimple in her left cheek that cut in so deeply, it looked like a comma. Her lips were full and painted with a light gold lip gloss that complimented her hair color. She was a class act. How she and Catherine became friends was a mystery. They didn't seem to have anything in common, but apparently they did.

Savonte' motioned for the waitress, and then ordered drinks for the ladies. Tony wanted the long legged, platinum fox and knew if he didn't move quickly Savonte' would scoop her up. He struck up a quiet, intimate conversation with her, while turning slightly away from the others.

"So, pretty lady, what's your name?"

"Janella Kennedy."

"Tell me a little about yourself."

"That could be lengthy. What specifically would you like to know?"

"Where are you from? What do you do? That sorta stuff."

"I was born in Louisiana, grew up in California, went to college in New Jersey, lived in New York for several years then moved here a few years ago. I'm Executive Vice President of an advertising firm, single, no children," she rattled in warp speed. "And you?" she said calmly as she took a sip of her drink.

Although Tony controlled his excitement, he was jumping for joy on the inside. *Hmmm, what a catch.* He got it together then responded, "I'm a native of Chicago, own an investment business, divorced and have one adult child. I'm quite taken by you. Would you like to go to dinner sometime?"

"Sure, why not."

Evan, Savonte' and Catherine had a side bar conversation going, but all three were tuned into Janella and Tony's conversation. Before Tony could respond to Janella they turned toward Tony, blatantly gawking down his throat, eager to hear what he had to say.

"Here's my card. Do you have one?"

Janella reached into her purse, then handed Tony one of her cards. Tony tapped it on the table before sticking it in his pocket. He gave her a wink then turned his attention back to the group. They were all engaged in a conversation about a number of subjects that they discussed through two more rounds of drinks. Evan's cell phone rang and it was apparent that the call was important.

"Tony, we need to leave right away."

Since Tony had ridden with Evan, he felt the need to leave as well. Tony told Janella he'd give her a call, then they both bid the ladies and Savonte' a good night.

After the number of drinks they'd all had, Catherine and Janella were ready to leave as well. Savonte' walked them out, but he went in the opposite direction to his car. Catherine reached her car first and offered to drive Janella to her car. Janella told her, "Thanks, but it's only a block away. I'm good." She strolled along, swinging her purse with every stride. As she approached the parking garage a man approached her. He was coming from another direction, but was the same distance from the parking gate as she was. At that moment, Janella wished she'd had Catherine drive her. A feeling of uncertainty came over her as they got closer, but to her pleasant surprise, it was Savonte'.

"Well, well Janella. If I'd known you were parked here, we could have walked together."

"That would have been nice, but I guess it's a mute point now."

Simultaneously, they asked each other; "What level are you parked on?"

They both chuckled a little then Janella responded, "On two."

"I'm on six. I can drive you to your car."

"That's not necessary; I'm just one flight up. I'm going to take the stairs. You can walk up with me if you'd like."

Savonte' nodded then extended his arm towards the stairwell. Janella's outfit was a long, linen, tan colored, wrap skirt, with a matching jacket that zipped in the front. With every step she took on the stairs, her skirt opened, exposing bare leg for what seemed to be miles on her long, five foot, eight inch frame. As they rounded the curve to the next set of stairs, Janella stopped on the landing, backing into the corner. She reached out, pulling Savonte' by the lapel on his jacket. She didn't have to pull too hard, as Savonte' was eager to get next to her. With fingers spread, she gripped his face and forcefully pulled his face to connect with hers. She kissed him so passionately, there was no way he would have resisted her. She was all over him, with the full intent of getting him to satisfy her craving for him. He ever so slowly and gently opened her wrapped skirt, revealing her lace panties and garter belt. While he stimulated the lower half of her body, she began to disrobe her upper half, exposing her perky breasts and hard nipples when she unzipped her jacket. The scent of her perfume drew him to her chest. He sucked her breast as though he was feeding for the first time. While he pleasured her breast, he drifted into la-la land. He seemed to drift there whenever he was sexually stimulated by someone who piqued his sexual curiosity. Janella stroked him until he was ready to take his ride. She braced herself against the wall and wrapped her legs around his waist, as he lifted her into the ideal position. She shrilled as he awakened the energy that had been bottled up. Even though Cynthia fulfilled Savonte', Janella's aura created a fanciful invigoration that excited him.

While he pulsated inside of her, she let out a scream. He held her buttocks in position with one hand, and then covered her mouth with the other hand to muffle the sound. She then opened her mouth and proceeded to suck his fingers, one-by-one. The vacuum action to his fingers was extremely erotic. To his surprise, the sounds were now coming from him. At that point, he dismounted, dropped to his knees and performed cunnilingus on her. The act sent Janella soaring beyond the peak of ecstasy. She released the grip of the fabric wadded in her hand, allowing her skirt to fall into place as it covered the upper half of his body. Her nails scraped the wall, and after almost losing her footing, she scuffed her Cole Haan loafers, as he took her to the height of orgasmic sensation.

When he finished, they straightened themselves and proceeded up the steps. As they approached Janella's car, she turned to Savonte' and they both started laughing.

"You're nasty." she said, as she grinned from ear to ear.

"You're just as nasty. You liked it."

Janella took a seat in her car, started the motor, blew him a kiss and pulled off.

Savonte' stood there, marveling at what had just taken place.

What the hell. With Cynthia broken in a million places, Janella can keep me pleasured. It's no big deal; a piece of ass is a piece of ass. Huh, they both do me incredibly well, so the trade off ain't so bad, he thought lustfully.

Savonte' went to his car and headed for home.

CHAPTER EIGHT

8

"The next morning, Savonte' reached the hospital

about nine-forty five. The attorney and the banker got there a little after ten o'clock. Cynthia was awake and a lot less groggy than the day before. Although she was still a bit hazy from the anesthesia the day before, she was still in agreement to let Savonte' handle her affairs while she was laid up. She verbally gave her permission as the banker signed off on the documents. The banker notarized the document, and then the attorney and the banker left.

Cynthia had Savonte' get her keys and her checkbook from her purse.

"I'm trusting you to handle my business and I hope you don't let me down."

"I can shred these papers right now if you're having second thoughts."

"I'm giving you complete control of all my possessions. You mean to tell me if the situation was reversed you wouldn't say the same thing?"

"I guess I would, but I want you to be comfortable that you've made the right decision. Would you rather Ardelia handle your affairs?"

"I trust Ardelia with my life, but she'll have enough on her plate caring for me and Chris."

"So, you're sure you're okay with this?"

Cynthia shook her head up and down then turned her face away from Savonte'. They sat in silence for a few minutes, then Savonte' told her he'd leave and let her have some space.

"I'll see you later," he said softly, as he kissed her forehead.

In the hallway, a man was being wheeled back to his room in a wheelchair. As their eyes met, Savonte' felt his heart skip a beat. He stood in place for several minutes before his rubbery legs would move. He proceeded in the direction of the wheeled man. He hovered around the outside of the room until the orderly left. The room was two doors down and across the hall from Cynthia. Savonte' looked around before entering the room.

"What the fuck are you doing here?" he asked the man in the bed.

"I was in a car accident."

"You're pretty jacked up. Did the others involved survive?"

"Yeah. I was told she survived, and since you're here, I would say that confirms what I was told."

Savonte' paused for a moment as he searched his thoughts.

"You're the one who crashed into Cynthia?"

"Yep. Are you upset with me, boss?"

"How did it happen? What were you thinking?"

"I was following her as you instructed me to do. She was driving like a race car driver and I lost control as we weaved in and out of the lanes."

"We need to get you out of here quickly."

"The doctors say it'll be weeks before I can leave."

"Oh, I don't think so. You can't be in here with her. There are too many unanswered questions, and you don't need to be within reaching distance."

"I can barely walk. There's no way I can walk out of here."

"I'll make the necessary arrangements, and you, my friend, should just go with the flow."

"I don't know man. I am pretty bad off right now."

"Either you follow my lead or you'll leave in a body bag. Which would you prefer?"

Blade turned his head to gaze out the window. Savonte' took his lack of response as a yes. In Savonte's mind, Blade was in agreement to be moved. Savonte' left the room on a mission, so preoccupied he didn't check the hallway before exiting the room. As he turned into the hallway he bumped into Ardelia and Chris. Ardelia nudged Chris on the shoulder, ushering her into Cynthia's room. Ardelia stayed back to talk to Savonte'.

"You know someone else who's in here?" she snarled.

"I went the wrong way when I came out of Cynthia's room."

"That didn't answer my question."

She put her hands on her hips and tapped her foot, awaiting his answer. However, her bold display of intimidation didn't move Savonte' in the least.

"And you expect me to answer you because...?"

They stared each other down, both refusing to give into the other. Savonte' placed one hand in his pants pocket and gaited down the hallway.

Ardelia was so irritated with him she was near eruption. She watched him until he was out of sight, then she went into Cynthia's room. She tried to suck up her anger so it wouldn't show on her face, but it didn't work with Cynthia. She picked up on it as soon as Ardelia stepped into the room. Ardelia didn't realize how much her voice had carried from the hallway. Cynthia detected the tone they'd used and knew there was an issue. Cynthia didn't say anything about what she'd overheard when Ardelia first came in because she wanted to hear all about Chris' trip first.

Chris didn't go into a lot of detail about the trip because she was more concerned about her mom. While Chris sat in the chair next to her mother's bed, she stretched her arms across Cynthia's body then laid her head on her stomach. As they hugged, Cynthia cut her eyes over to Ardelia. Ardelia pulled up another chair and sat next to the bed, too. Chris raised her head inquiring, "I'm going to the cafeteria. Does anybody want a soda or something?"

"No, I can't have anything right now," Cynthia responded. Ardelia shook her head, indicating no.

The moment Chris left the room, Cynthia questioned Ardelia.

"What was going on in the hallway between you and Savonte'?"

"I saw him coming out of the room across the hall, but he wouldn't explain who else he was here to see."

"And why should he? Why would you feel the need to interrogate him?"

"Because something didn't feel right to me. The question was harmless, so why did he get so huffy?"

"It's the principal of the thing, the mere fact that you were questioning him probably made his defenses go up. Come on Ardelia, you would have reacted the same way if the situation were reversed."

"Yes, I probably would have, but I smell a rat where he's concerned and it stinks to high hell."

"Ardelia, he's never done anything to cause you to be suspicious of him. Chill out okay?"

"Okay, I'll keep my suspicions to myself, for now anyway."

"Good."

"So what was he doing here so early?"

Cynthia rolled her eyes, knowing that Ardelia was not going to take the news very well, but she figured that now was as good a time as any.

"Since your hands will be so full with Chris and me intruding in your life, Savonte' is going to handle my business affairs. He brought some documents for me to have notarized."

"HE'S GOING TO DO WHAT???!! YOU DID WHAT?!!"

"Calm down, Ardelia. I didn't want you to have to do everything."

"CYNTHIA! Why can't you see there's something clandestine about him! Certainly you can see beyond his looks and what's hanging in his pants, can't you?"

"Of course I can, but I don't see the picture you're trying to paint. I think you're a little premature and unreasonable in your skepticism."

"Oh sure...you're so fucking astute, nothing can get past you, right?"

"Ardelia, I don't have the energy to be bothered with your nonsense."

"Oh really now?"

Chris walked back into the room, preventing Ardelia from saying anything else. Ardelia scooted her chair backward, scraping the chair legs on the polyurethane floor. She sprung from the chair, clutching her purse under her arm, told Chris she'd meet her in the car, then stormed out of the room.

"What happened in here while I was gone?" Chris questioned.

"Nothing for you to be concerned about. Don't even feel it,

it's nothing we can't get through."

Chris shrugged her shoulders, took a swig of her soda and then sat down.

Once Ardelia made it to the elevator, she turned around and headed back down the hallway. She slowed her pace as she neared Cynthia's room. She darted past Cynthia's doorway without being seen and proceeded to the room Savonte' had been in. She peeked in to see who was in there. The man was asleep, so she tiptoed in. She didn't see anything visible that would give her any indication of what his connection was to Savonte', so she turned to leave. As she got to the doorway, he opened his eyes asking Ardelia in a whisper, "Who are you?"

"I uh, came into the wrong room, sorry."

"What are you up to, lady?"

Ardelia decided that the only way to find out the connection with Savonte' was to ask questions. Therefore, she returned to the man's bedside to see what she could find out.

"What are you really doing in here?"

"Do you drive a silver, Infinity S.U.V.?"

Without thinking he responded, "Yes, well, I did until I killed it the other day."

"My girlfriend is the one you had the accident with."

Ardelia thought for a second that she should spin it in a positive way so that he wouldn't feel threatened.

"Well, it's good you both made it out alive. I know she'll

want to know that you're okay. When she's able to get out of bed, I'm sure she'd like to meet you. From the looks of the both of you, you'll be here for a while. Have the doctors said how long you have to stay?"

He could tell he was being baited and he realized he'd already said too much. *I'll be gone soon, so I'll feed you a taste*, he thought.

"Sure, you guys can visit anytime. Let her know I'm glad she survived."

"So, have the doctors said how long you'll be here?"

"Nope."

He kept opening and closing his eyes, pretending to be dozing off. Ardelia caught on, thanked him for his time then turned to leave. She stopped at the door and asked; "So what's your name?"

"Just call me Blade."

"All right" she responded as she turned to leave.

Shit this is as critical as Savonte' suspected. He has to get me out of here now, Blade thought to himself in a panic.

By the time Ardelia made it to her car, Chris was approaching the car, too. Chris had many questions on the drive home. Ardelia was guarded with her answers, but answered Chris the best she could without saying too much. She knew something fishy was going on, but didn't have enough pieces to complete the puzzle. She definitely didn't want Chris to be worried or concerned, so she kept her answers short and sweet. Cynthia had boarded another runaway train, and

Ardelia was not about to let Chris get hit by it again. She was committed to protecting Chris from her mother's stupid ass choices. Chris got a call on her cell phone, which allowed Ardelia to become absorbed in thought. *From the moment Cynthia met this man, she's been different. She's always defending Savonte' and can't see further than her own fucking nose where he's concerned. She acts like a gullible schoolgirl. As sure as my name is Ardelia, he poses a threat to her. Somehow, I'm going to figure out what the hell his motives are. He's a slime bucket masked by fine clothes, a body to die for and a face that would make you drop your panties on sight. To top it off, he has her addicted to sex with him. I have been with her through every ounce of bullshit, with every motherfucker who has fucked over her. There's no way, I'll bail on her now. Her disappointments and emotional pain have left so many scars that she's emotionally on her last leg. One more dagger is sure to flatten her. I'll be damned,* Ardelia's mind raced.

They were a few blocks from the house when Chris hung up from her call. Chris saw a fast food restaurant, pointing for Ardelia to go through the drive through. Chris was grabbing for fries before Ardelia took her hand off the bag.

"Hungry are you?"

With her jaws chugged full of French fries, Chris replied, "Yep."

"Girl, you eat like you work construction. One day you won't be able to eat like that and keep your waistline." Chris kept stuffing her face as if Ardelia hadn't said anything. When they got to the house, they went to their bedrooms.

Ardelia lay across the bed, sick over what had transpired at the hospital. She had no clue how to get Cynthia to open her eyes and she knew if she kept ragging on Savonte', Cynthia would only get closer to him. Keeping her mouth shut to all the bullshit going on around her would be the ultimate task. However, she sure as hell was going to keep her eyes open, and then speak when she had facts to back it up. Her life was already hectic, and now with Chris and Cynthia coming to live with her, she was going to have her hands even more full. She had no idea how she'd get the facts she needed, and playing Sherlock was not in her career plans. She reached over to the night stand and clicked on the compact disc player. She rolled over onto her back and stared at the ceiling, while she listened to some jazz. The soothing music relaxed her and she drifted off to sleep. While Ardelia slept, Chris blasted her music, danced and talked on the phone.

An hour or so into Ardelia's nap, she heard a rattle at the patio door. Just as she went to check to make sure it was locked, the door was jerked and came sliding open. "So you think you can step in and fuck up my life with Cynthia, huh?" Savonte' grabbed Ardelia by the throat and slammed her against the wall. As he released his grip, he warned her to stop asking questions. She swallowed hard and proceeded to scream.

Ardelia yelled at the top of her lungs. Chris had just turned off her stereo when she heard Ardelia screaming. She raced down the hallway and burst into Ardelia's bedroom.

"What's wrong, Aunt Ardelia?"

Ardelia was holding her throat and gasping for air.

"I must have been dreaming that someone broke in through the patio door and tried to kill me," she explained.

"Yeah, you had to be dreaming, 'cause the patio doors are downstairs and you've been in here the entire time."

Ardelia got out of the bed, went to the bathroom and splashed cold water on her face.

"Are you all right, Auntie?"

"I'm good. You can go back to your room."

Chris went back to her room and flopped on the bed. *Everybody around me is crazy. Damn, I'll be glad when I can get a place of my own. Nothing has been normal since my dad died. My mom is not the same and it seems like she's coming unglued. If she and Aunt Ardelia think they're fooling me, they're not. I know something's up that they don't want me to know about. I just don't want to go through, what I did before getting mixed up in my mom's drama,"* Chris thought in desperation.

Ring, Ring, Ring.

"Hello? Hello?" Ardelia and Chris answered at the same time.

"Hey, you two, what cha doing?" Cynthia murmured into the phone.

"Hey, Mom, I'm lying on the bed and Aunt Ardelia was too. How you feelin'?"

"Bout the same, but hanging in there. I just wanted to check up on you and talk to Ardelia."

"Okay, I'll see you tomorrow."
There was a click, indicating Chris had dropped from the call.

"Ardelia, I just wanted to apologize for the way I talked to you earlier. I know you have my best interests at heart."

There were moments of silence before Ardelia decided to speak. She loved her friend, but she was really pissed at how dense Cynthia was acting.

"I'm going to say this, then I'm done preaching, but you need to hear what I have to say."

"Ardelia..."

"Shut up and listen. I told you when you first met Savonte' to take it slow. There's something about him I don't like and after that stunt today, I'm more convinced. Right now I can't get you to see anything wrong, but promise me if you get in too far over your head, you'll let me help you."

Cynthia absorbed what Ardelia had to say then responded, "I won't challenge you because I know if I needed you, you'd be there for me."

"Enough said then. Love you. See you tomorrow."

After they hung up, Cynthia made up her mind to pay very close attention to Savonte'. *Maybe I'm too involved to see anything wrong. It's possible I could be getting suckered, but it doesn't feel like that. I won't change my attitude, but I'll pay closer attention.*

Ardelia, on the other hand, was strategizing in her head. She felt she needed to be sneaky to get the goods on the bastard. She lived a pretty solid, drama free life, but her past was full of turbulence and turmoil. It would take a little reaching back into her bag of old tricks, but she was certain she'd come up with something.

Meanwhile, the clock was a ticking, bringing the day to a close. Ardelia and Chris ate a quiet dinner then returned to their bedrooms for the night.

CHAPTER NINE

9

T he crashing of thunder and the sound of golf ball sized

hail beat against the window as the morning light broke into Ardelia's bedroom window. Chris slept through the commotion, unaware of the storm. Ardelia heard the ruckus, but wasn't ready to start her day. She curled up into a ball and pulled the covers over her head. Her internal clock said it was time to rise, so no matter how tightly she squinted or how firm she buried her head in the pillow, she could not go back to sleep. She had wrestled with her subconscious state of mind all night anyway, and the storm merely added to her inability to relax. Frustrated and perturbed she sharply flung the covers and got out of the bed. She went ahead and made the bed before making coffee.

While she was making coffee, the phone rang. Cynthia was calling to check on them, since the news had reported pockets of flooding throughout the surrounding areas. She told Ardelia not to try to make it to the hospital today. They didn't need another tragedy to deal with. Ardelia agreed, but was reluctant. She wanted to spend some more time with Blade, to squeeze some information out of him. She figured that missing one day wasn't that big of a deal. As banged up as Blade was, he'd be there when she went back. She and Cynthia chatted a little while about insignificant topics until they couldn't stomach the strain any longer.

Ardelia poured a cup of coffee, sat at the kitchen table and looked out onto the down pouring of rain. She was bored stiff since she'd taken time off of her job for Chris and Cynthia. The boredom was too much to deal with, so she called into her office to see what was going on.

She then decided to take advantage of her down time and read a book she'd bought a few days before. She went upstairs, showered and put on a silk pajama set. She returned downstairs and fixed another cup of coffee. She got out the book from the book shelf and her throw blanket and then curled up on the sofa.

After reading the first three chapters, she was glad that she had taken the time to open it. It had piqued her interest in such a way, she couldn't put it down. The sound of the rain, peace and quiet and a good book made for the perfect day.

While Ardelia read, Chris slept. Chris was the typical teenager, not interested in getting out of bed before noon. Ardelia took advantage of that and became more and more enthralled in her book. She spent several, much needed, restful hours on the sofa reading, until Chris awakened.

For some reason, Chris wanted to talk about her mother. She went as far as going down memory lane. She talked about her fondest memories, their fights and even times with her dad. She reminisced as if her mother had died. Ardelia allowed Chris to express herself without interjecting her thoughts or opinions. What took Ardelia by surprise was the fact that Chris told Ardelia that she wanted to live with her until she graduated from high school. Well, that sure got Ardelia's attention. She could no longer keep her mouth shut. She had to pick Chris' brain. She really needed to understand what was going on with her.

"Chris, you know that you and your mom can stay here as long as you need to."

"I know, but I mean after my mom gets better and is able to move out, I want to stay with you."

"I don't mind you staying with me, but clearly I can't make that decision without your mother's input."

"Why not? She doesn't know I exist half the time."

"That's not true and you know it," Ardelia snapped.

Why am I defending Cynthia when this child is dead on? Ardelia pondered.

"Aunt Ardelia, my mom hasn't been the same since my dad died. I thought when we moved and went through that craziness with Thomas that we would get close again. Most of the time she treats me like I'm grown and I have to deal with everything without her anyway. I love my mom, you know I do, but I think she has some stuff to deal with and I honestly feel like I'm in the way." Ardelia was floored.

"Why don't we talk to your mom when she gets released? Let's see how we can mend things back together for the two of you."

"Nope, not interested in mending. As soon as I believe in her, she lets me down. It was never that way before, but she's changed. I still want to go to college, but my grades dropped, 'cause I'm always trippin', on something that's going on with her. If she changes she'll have to change because she wants to, not for me.

Ardelia pulled Chris in close to her. As independent and cocky as Chris might be most of the time, she was still young enough to want and need her mother. The conversation made Ardelia sick to her stomach, especially since she'd already warned Cynthia to consider how her actions would impact Chris.

Cynthia needs her ass kicked, but until she recognizes there's a problem, it won't do any good. This is such a messed up situation. We have to get back to normal, Ardelia thought.

The things Chris shared with Ardelia put a halt to her reading her book. Her mind was so preoccupied she wouldn't retain anything she read. She put her bookmark in the book and returned it to the bookcase. Now that Chris had unleashed her feelings, it was obvious she was feeling pretty needy. It was like a huge wall Chris had built around herself had come crumbling down. She felt vulnerable and wanted a sense of security. The only one who could give her that right now was Ardelia. Although Ardelia didn't have any children, she had a loving nature about her that Chris really needed. They went upstairs and Chris wanted to stay in Ardelia's room. Chris lay across Ardelia's legs while Ardelia polished her nails. It was so obvious that Chris was relaxed. They laughed and talked as they hadn't in a long time. Chris was telling funny stories and cracking jokes. They were really enjoying each other, but it made Ardelia a little uncomfortable. She could tell that Chris was settling in, but she didn't want her to get too comfortable until she knew that Cynthia was on board with letting Chris stay. Chris probably figured if her mother saw how happy she was, she'd agree. Her thought process could be dead on, but if she was wrong, she'd be worse off.

The rain soon subsided and Chris and Ardelia scrambled to get out of the house. They jumped in the car and headed for the mall. They window shopped for hours, until Chris happened upon an outfit that she was willing to die for. Chris screeched and jumped up and down, until Ardelia gave in and bought it. That was the climax of Chris' day, but Ardelia wanted to eat. They moseyed down the mall into a restaurant, where Ardelia flopped down in the booth, ordering appetizers as soon as she was handed a menu. Chris' appetite was suppressed the moment the sales clerk put her outfit in the bag. She perused the menu and decided on a light entree. Shortly after the soft drinks arrived, Ardelia's appetizer plate was placed in front of her. She was chewing so fast and breathing so hard, you would've thought she hadn't eaten in a week. Chris buried her face in her hand, embarrassed by Ardelia's slightly barbaric table etiquette.

By the time Ardelia realized how uncivilized she was acting, she had scarfed down most of the food on her plate. Chris peeked at her through of her fingers to see if it was safe to uncover her face. Ardelia was patting her mouth with her napkin when she noticed Chris peeking at her through her fingers. She smiled widely, and they both burst into laughter.

"Dang, you were real hungry, huh?"

"Yep, and ready for more."

Just as she completed her sentence, their entrees arrived. Ardelia clapped her hands and rubbed them together in sheer delight. Chris rolled her eyes as she dug into her food.

"Please, Missy, you have a lot of nerve acting like you're ashamed of me. I didn't run and hide when you performed in the store for that outfit, did I?"

"But I wasn't acting like you."

"No, you were acting like you, and believe me, you were just as dramatic, so stop acting so damn high and mighty now."

"Okay, okay, sorry."

Since Ardelia was still famished, she hastily completed her meal. After they finished, they headed back to the house.

Once they were back in the house, Chris reverted back to the needy little girl she'd been before they left the house. They hung out in Ardelia's bedroom and watched movies until they both fell asleep. Ardelia was only able to get in a wink or two. During the course of the night, she had trouble sleeping. She was anxious to talk to Blade.

She tossed and turned until she became frustrated. She got out of bed and piddled around the house. The night seemed to linger on and on. There was no glimpse of dawn, so she pulled her book off the shelf and picked up where she had left off earlier in the day. She managed to read four chapters before light emerged on the window. She didn't want to awaken Chris too early, so she read a few more chapters before waking her.

They ate breakfast, dressed and left for the hospital. All the way down the highway, Ardelia mentally rehearsed the questions she had for Blade. More than anything, she wanted to prove to Cynthia that this Savonte' character was foul.

When they walked into the hospital, Ardelia made a big deal about needing a soda. She wanted to go to Blade's room without Cynthia or Chris knowing. She told Chris to go on ahead to Cynthia's room and she'd be there shortly. Ardelia left Chris at the elevator and walked in the direction of the cafeteria. After making her way down the hallway, she took the stairs up to the third floor. The stairwell door was next to Blade's room. She peeked into the hallway to make sure the coast was clear. She eased out into the hallway then slipped into Blade's room. Unfortunately, there was no one in the room. She stood around for a bit, anticipating Blade's return. Those few minutes seemed like an eternity. With her hands clinched tightly, she twisted and turned in a circle. Eventually, she decided to take a look around the room. She opened drawers and the closet, but there was no sign of Blade's existence. As she turned to leave, an orderly came into the room. On sight of each other they stopped in their tracks.

"Can I help you?" the orderly asked.

"I was here to see Blade. Do you know when he'll be back?"

"He's gone. He was transferred out this morning."

"Transferred? Transferred where?"

"I don't know. I'm just here to change the linen."

Ardelia shook her head and stormed out of the room. It was just her luck that Savonte' was on his way to Cynthia's room and he saw her coming out of Blade's room. Ardelia looked up and directly into Savonte's eyes. He gave her a guileful smirk, before locking in on a cold, hard stare. Ardelia didn't want Cynthia to be upset by any friction, so she nodded to Savonte' and went into Cynthia's room wearing a smile.

Savonte' walked into the room, shaking his keys in his hand. He spoke to Chris, then leaned over the bed and kissed Cynthia. Since Chris didn't know Savonte', she had an inquisitive look on her face as she sat back in her chair to observe him. Cynthia's focus and attention immediately turned to Savonte'. Chris was disappointed and Ardelia was livid as she watched Cynthia practically ignore them for the likes of Savonte'.

Savonte' dominated the conversation and kept Cynthia completely engaged in conversation. After making several unsuccessful attempts to participate in their conversation, Ardelia stood to look out the window. Her folded arms and tapping foot made it clear to everyone in the room that she was irritated. Chris repeatedly let out sighs of hot air. Between the two of them they made Savonte' and Cynthia uncomfortable.

Savonte' kissed Cynthia and left the room without a farewell to Chris or Ardelia. Needless to say, Cynthia was not happy with her friend or her daughter. She ripped into them for their rude, inconsiderate behavior. While Chris sat and took her scolding, Ardelia rebutted with vicious, wicked words that made them all pause. The words were out and there was no way to take them back. Although she felt like shit for causing her friend pain, she believed what she'd said was right and felt she needed to hear it.

As Cynthia straightened up in the bed, tears streamed down her face. After Ardelia's tirade, Chris knew better than to voice her opinion. She sat still and patiently waited to see how her mom and Ardelia would hash it out.

Ardelia's jaws were clinched tightly, while Cynthia's jaws swelled with air. She let out a sigh then immediately lashed out at Ardelia.

"Ardelia, you can take your insults and get the fuck out of here!"

"Insults! Insults! How the hell can you be insulted by what I said? Is there anything that I said that wasn't true? I haven't called you out of your name or accused you of doing anything you haven't done. I am merely pointing out facts and trying to get you to open your eyes to a different perspective. Why can't you try to understand?"

"Understand? Understand that you see me as a stupid, mindless twit?"

"I never said, nor implied anything like that and you know it. You're twisting my words."

"Bullshit, Ardelia. Stop pretending that you weren't trying to hurt me."

"That's not true. Just take the time to think about what I said. Be open and objective to my point of view."

"What a bright, fucking idea! Fuck you, and your fucking point of view."

As Ardelia puckered her lips to respond, Cynthia flicked her wrist, indicating she could leave, then turned to face the wall. Chris got up from the chair where she was sitting, leaned over, kissed her mom and then followed Ardelia out of the room.

Ardelia was enraged, so she swiftly moved down the hallway, swinging her arms and blowing out heavy sighs with every step. Chris moved much slower, dragging her feet, and her head was pointed toward the floor.

When Ardelia reached the car, she noticed that Chris was no where around. As she started to panic, Chris came walking out of the door. Ardelia flopped into the driver's seat and sat with the door open until Chris reached the car. As she turned the key in the ignition, she suddenly realized that she hadn't gotten any information on where Blade had been moved. She pressed her back against the seat, extended her arms and tightly gripped the steering wheel. She quickly realized that she couldn't get any information on a man named Blade. Surely, the hospital records wouldn't have "Blade" entered into the computer. Savonte' was the 'big fish' she wanted to get the goods on, anyway. She pulled herself together, put the car in gear and headed for home.

The ride home was a little tense, but Ardelia and Chris got through it. As they pulled into the driveway, Chris gave a quick glance towards Ardelia out of the corner of her eye. Ardelia could sense that Chris wanted to talk, so as they walked up to the house, she asked," What's on your mind, Chris?"

"Well, uh, I want to stay with you now more than ever. After watching my mom with Savonte', I know I don't want to be with her until she's the way she used to be. I just can't deal with her right now."

As the tears streamed down Chris' face, Ardelia pulled her close and hugged her.

"It's going to be all right Chris. Just hang on."
Chris looked up at her and asked, "So can I please stay with you?"

"Okay, but if your mom objects, I can't override her."

"All right, it's a deal. We don't have to say anything to her, until the time comes, all right?"

Ardelia nodded in agreement, as they went to their bedrooms. Chris undressed and showered, while Ardelia soaked in her bathtub. Ardelia was overwhelmed by what had taken place at the hospital, and knowing that she'd just agreed to take on the role of mother, unbeknownst to her best friend, made her sick. She had no problem with taking Chris in, but she wondered what strain she, and Cynthia would have to endure during the process. She brought her knees up close to her chest and rested her chin on her knees. She sat in the tub thinking for so long, the bath water turned cold.

When she returned to her bedroom, she found Chris stretched across her bed.

"Can I sleep with you again?" Chris pleaded.

"Sure, why not."

Although Ardelia didn't mind Chris sleeping with her, she didn't have the energy to have any discussions. She hoped that Chris would not strike up a conversation. By the time she'd brushed her teeth, moisturized her body and put on her pajamas, Chris was sound asleep.

CHAPTER TEN

10

Ardelia was awakened by the ringing of the telephone.

"Hello?" she answered in a low, dry tone.

"Ardelia, wake up. The doctor is releasing me today."

"Releasing you? Already?"

"Yes, I have to go to therapy but it beats being here."

"What time do I need to pick you up?"

"You don't have to come get me. The doctor has made arrangements to have me brought home. I just wanted to make sure you would be there."

"Do I need to do anything special to accommodate you?"

"No, but may I ask to use the bedroom downstairs? Climbing the stairs won't be an easy thing to do for a while."

"I wish I'd had more notice. I haven't used that room for a bedroom in a long time. It's been a catch all room for so long, I'll

have to clean it out first."

"I'm sorry it's such short notice, but I had no control."

"Don't worry about it. I'll get up and start cleaning. What time do you expect to be here?"

"I'd say about one-thirty."

"It'll be ready. Let me go get started."

When they hung up, Ardelia slid out of bed and mumbled to herself all the way downstairs.

Damn it. Keep my fucking point of view huh? Now a day later, I have to get up at the fucking crack of dawn to clean out a room for your ignorant ass. If I didn't love you, as if you were my sister, I'd let them sit your crippled ass on a street corner," Ardelia said aloud to herself. She clicked on the light in the spare room, snarled and put her hands on her hips. The sight of the work she had cut out for her caused her to talk to herself again.

Shit. What have I signed up for? This is three days of work that I'll have to get done in a few hours. The shit I go through for you, Ms. I don't want to hear what you have to say. I should choke you until you understand my fucking point of view.

She kept mumbling, while moving shit around for hours. In her mind she hadn't made a lot of progress, but when Chris appeared in the doorway, she commented how nice the room looked.

"What made you do this?"

Ardelia whirled around, and sharply responded, "Your mother will be here in a few hours."

"Oh," Chris said, with a twinge of an attitude.

"Oh? What's the attitude about?"

"I just don't feel up to dealing with her drama. I'm happy that she's doing better, but I was getting used to peace and quiet. When she gets here it'll be more like yesterday.

"Yesterday is behind us. Give her a chance. Let's try to make this work, okay?"

"All right. Want some help?

Ardelia and Chris cleaned and rearranged furniture for another hour before taking a break to eat. Not long after they finished eating and returned to finish up the room, the doorbell rang.

The medical vehicle had arrived with Cynthia. They brought her in and she hobbled to the sofa in the family room. Given Cynthia's condition and the circumstances, it should have been a warm reception. However, there was a feeling of uneasiness that lingered throughout the house. Cynthia was still miffed from the argument with Ardelia, Chris was uneasy because she couldn't express her true thoughts to her mom and the words *'Keep your fucking point of view'*, kept echoing in Ardelia's mind. For fear Cynthia would ask questions that she didn't want to answer, Chris stuck close to Ardelia. Whenever Ardelia left the room, Chris found a reason to leave. Naturally, Cynthia noticed how strangely Chris was behaving and became concerned. Cynthia and Chris had been separated for weeks since Chris had been on vacation with her friend, but Cynthia could feel a serious disconnect and it hit her pretty hard.

Cynthia wasn't willing to lose the closeness they'd always shared, but she had no clue what was going on with her daughter. Therefore, she didn't know how to fix it. She sat and pondered over the dilemma until pain swept through her body. She made her way to her bedroom and into the bed, popped a pain pill into her mouth and was asleep in no time.

Ardelia was able to free herself from Chris when Chris got a phone call from Lolly. Chris went to her room and talked to Lolly for hours. Ardelia had settled in comfortably and was watching a movie, but not long after she got into the most exciting part of the movie, Chris entered the room. Ardelia didn't want to shun her, but she really needed her space. She hadn't had any time alone, in what felt like forever, but she knew Chris needed her more than she needed her own space. She waved her in, but kept her eyes and her focus on the television. Chris seemed to be in tune with Ardelia's need for space, so she quietly crawled into the bed and watched the movie with her. Chris wasn't able to watch the movie to the end though. Her eyes glazed over and she drifted off to sleep.

Ardelia finished watching the movie and tuned right into the next one. The beginning of the movie captured her attention right from the start. Midway through the movie, she started drifting off to sleep. She was determined to see it to the end, so she sat up in the bed. Once the movie came to an end, she was glad that she hadn't missed it. She turned off the television and snuggled under the covers.

The night passed slowly, while Ardelia tossed and turned,

thinking about her new housemates. She was hoping that Chris and Cynthia would mend their relationship before Cynthia was able to move back to her house. She thought about how carefree her life was, and really wasn't ready for a teenager to put a kink in it. She turned over and watched Chris sleep. She slept so peacefully, it made Ardelia rethink her thoughts.

Why the hell has Cynthia fucked up her life again? Shit, she's fucked up Chris' life and mine. She'd better hurry up and get her act together. I didn't have children because I didn't want the responsibility. Now I have to instantly become a mother of a teenager . . . ugh." she thought.

Ardelia covered her face with the covers, drifting off into a deep sleep. By the time morning came, Chris was awake and downstairs with Cynthia. Ardelia dragged her tired, limp body down the steps and into the family room. She interrupted a tender moment between Cynthia and Chris that she felt uneasy about. It was apparent that they were sharing some much needed time, and for some odd reason Ardelia felt slighted and left out. Even though Ardelia knew Cynthia and Chris needed to find their way back to each other, last night she'd convinced herself that she could be good for Chris. She'd come to terms with having Chris live with her, but now it seemed like that wouldn't be happening.

Ardelia asked if they wanted breakfast, then she made her way to the kitchen. She clanged pots and pans, relieving her frustration while she cooked. She knew she should have been glad for the two of them, but she now wanted the chance to rescue Chris from Cynthia's destructive behavior. No matter how destructive Cynthia might be, she was still Chris' mother, and they should have the chance to repair their relationship. Ardelia finished preparing breakfast, serving Cynthia and Chris in the family room. She returned to the kitchen to get her plate, but decided to eat alone. As she took her last bite of toast, Chris came into the kitchen. Chris noticed the pitiful look on Ardelia's face and asked, "What's wrong?"

Ardelia raised her head and looked into Chris' innocent eyes, then choked on her words. She couldn't form a complete sentence, so she merely waved her hand, indicating nothing was wrong. Since Chris was high on bonding with her mom she said, "Okay." She placed the dishes in the sink and went back to visit with her mom.

Ardelia felt dismissed. She couldn't believe that Chris had become so different overnight. Whatever Cynthia had said to Chris, she had regained her trust and her love. It was very clear that the love they had for each other went beyond any feelings Chris may have had for Ardelia. Ardelia took a deep breath and sucked up the tears she felt whirling around inside of herself. She cleaned up the kitchen then headed back to her bedroom. She stopped at the foot of the stairs and watched Chris and Cynthia sitting closely together and laughing at a movie. She tilted her head back to keep the tears from dropping onto her face and proceeded up the steps. She walked into her closet, grabbed an outfit and a pair of shoes. She wanted to give Cynthia and Chris some time alone. She dressed then let them know she was going out for a while.

"Going out to spend money, girl?" Cynthia asked.

"I don't know, maybe," Ardelia replied, as she walked toward the front door. Chris kept her eyes glued to the television and waved her hand, but by the time she waved, Ardelia had her back to her, so she figured Chris had ignored her departure.

When the movie was almost over, a ringing was coming from Cynthia's purse.

"Is that my phone? Chris, hand me my purse, please." Reluctantly, Chris got the purse and sat it in Cynthia's lap.

"Hello," Cynthia answered.

"Hey, honey," a deep voice echoed from the other end of the phone.

"Savonte'?" Cynthia queried.

"Yes, it's me. How are you?"

Chris let out a sigh, pounded her fist on the sofa, rolled her eyes and stormed out of the room.

Cynthia hesitated before responding to Savonte' as she watched Chris leave the room.

"Hello, Cynthia, are you still there?"

"Yes, I'm here. I was distracted. What did you ask me?"

"I asked how you were."

"It's been days since I've heard from you. I could have been dead and buried and you would have missed the funeral. So was your question just a standard, canned question of concern?"

"No, it's not like that at all. You know your friend doesn't like me and I didn't know when would be the best time to call."

"That's bullshit. You could have called my cell as you just did. She wouldn't have answered my cell and you know it."

"Hey, I didn't call to argue. I..."

"Then why did you?"

"Where's the attitude coming from?"

"I haven't seen you, or talked to you but once since I gave you control of my business affairs, and now you call casually like it's no big deal. How would you feel?"

"Let's not do this, okay?"

Silence came over the phone as Cynthia carefully chose her words.

"I'm fine. So tell me how's my house and my financial affairs?"

"How are they?" he asked inquisitively.

"Yeah, is everything okay?"

"What could be wrong?"

"Now where's your attitude coming from?"

"I don't like being questioned. If you didn't think I was capable of handling your business, you should have had someone else take care of it for you."

"I'm really not up to this right now. Why don't we try this another time?"

Click...Cynthia quickly disconnected the call.

Needless to say, they both were a little upset with the other.

Savonte' sat and stewed, but only for a short time. He picked up the phone and called Janella. After they finished talking, Savonte' slipped on his shoes and left for Janella's house.

Meanwhile, Cynthia was disgusted with herself. *I knew the night Catherine and I ran into them at Syncopations that I should have put on the brakes. Why didn't I listen to my inner voice then?* She asked herself. She quickly realized how foolish she had been to entrust Savonte' with her financial affairs. At this point, she wanted nothing more than to take it all back. However, since she wasn't able to get around and the paperwork was already signed, she didn't think she had much leverage. She wanted to get back to the life she once knew, but she had to heal before she could do much of anything.

Chris was still in her bedroom, disappointed that Cynthia had allowed Savonte's call to interrupt their bonding. She had, once again, reverted back to feeling sad about being left out of her mother's life.

While Cynthia and Chris remained in their respective rooms, Ardelia came barreling through the door. When Chris heard the door slam, she raced down the steps. Ardelia was already in the family room telling Cynthia what she'd learned while she was out.

"I'm telling you Cynthia, it has to be the same guy."

"You think just overhearing two men talking about a man found dead that it's the guy who I was involved in the accident with?"

"How many men do you know named Blade? Damn, Cynthia, step out of that stupid ass fog you've been in and put your thinking cap back on."

Cynthia sat and stared at Ardelia for a few minutes, absorbing the realization of her stupidity. Although she thought earlier that she may have made a mistake, she wasn't ready to admit it to Ardelia. She felt a lump in her throat as she responded,

"Okay Ardelia, I get the picture. So how do we find out what's going on?"

Cynthia turned around and saw Chris standing in the doorway. Chris made her way into the room, but snuggled up next to Ardelia. Ardelia was taken aback since Chris and Cynthia were getting along so well before she left. They allowed Chris to stay in the room while they talked.

"The only name you have on this man is Blade. How do you track down Blade?"

"Since you had the accident with the man, I'm sure his real name is on the accident report. I seriously doubt that the motor vehicle department allowed Blade to be printed on his driver's license," Ardelia exclaimed.

"Okay, smart ass. I can't get out of the house for a couple of weeks to go pick up the accident report, so I guess we have to wait."

"The hell we do. Let's look on the computer and see if we can request the accident report to be mailed."

Ardelia went to the computer and logged onto the website. Luckily, she was right, but the report could only be mailed to the address of record and would take three to five business days. Ardelia returned to the sofa with pen in hand. She made a list of things to do for the next five days. Now that Ardelia had gotten Cynthia thinking clearly, she was convinced she could get to the bottom of Savonte's intentions. After making her list, she headed up to her bedroom.

A short time later, Chris emerged in Ardelia's doorway. She had a sorrowful look about her, which tugged on Ardelia's heartstrings. She opened her arms wide, encouraging Chris to come into the room. After a while, Chris felt comfortable and scooted over to the other side of the bed. Ardelia turned out the lights and darkness filled the entire house. Chris quickly went to sleep, while Ardelia lay in the darkness, anxiously awaiting the next day.

CHAPTER ELEVEN

11

O n the other side of town, Savonte' comfortably

lounged in Janella's bed. Contrary to being the usual man in control, Janella was leading him around by the nose. He couldn't believe how he did whatever she asked him to whenever she asked him to do it. He was so busy trying to impress her, he had already used some of Cynthia's money to buy her gifts.

Savonte' was irritated by Cynthia questioning him about her financial affairs because he knew that in the little time he'd had access to her accounts, he'd depleted a big chunk of her money. As a matter of fact, he hadn't paid one bill or gone to the house to make sure everything was still intact. All he knew was that he couldn't get enough of Janella and he would do whatever he had to in order to keep spending time with her. Yeah, he was a suave, good looking and ruthless business man, but Janella had put him under a spell that he couldn't seem to shake.

When Janella graced the bedroom in a pair of red lace shorts and tank top, Savonte' was up, literally, for anything she was ready and willing to do. Foreplay was to the second power, which created so much electrical energy, they were damn near scorched. They pleasured each other until the sun came up.

The next morning Janella wanted more, more than just sex that is. She had seen some new furniture that she was dying to have, but didn't want to spend her own money to get it. By the time they'd finished their morning lovemaking, Savonte' had offered to buy her whatever she wanted.

Janella rolled over, grinning slyly, as she made her way to the bathroom. Savonte' positioned his hands behind his head, perched up as though he was a king. Little did he know Janella was playing him as easily as she played the piano.

After Janella showered, she returned to the bedroom with clean sheets. While Savonte' showered and freshened up, Janella tidied up the bedroom and got dressed. She was all spiffed up and ready to shop. She wasn't hungry for breakfast and certainly not interested in cooking. Savonte' hinted a couple of times that he was hungry, so after the third hint, Janella suggested that they go to the restaurant near the furniture store. Savonte' was not happy with the suggestion, but realized he wouldn't eat if he didn't go, so to the restaurant it was.

On the ride into town Janella attempted small talk, but the only responses she got were occasional grunts. Janella knew she'd let the air out of his ego and she needed to somehow pump it back up.

She knew the edge she had on him was sex, so she put her creative juices to work. She had to do him before they got back to her place. Savonte' pulled in front of the restaurant and parked. As he put one hand on the handle to open his door, Janella placed one hand on her forehead and the other on her stomach. Savonte' got out of the car, walked around to the passenger's side and opened her door. He kneeled down eye level to her.

"What's wrong?" he asked softly.

"All of a sudden I feel hot and nauseous."

"What can I do?"

"I just need to get to the ladies' room. Let's go into the restaurant."

Savonte' helped her inside and walked her to the ladies' room. He returned to the front to be seated. He ordered a cup of coffee while he looked over the menu. After deciding what he wanted, he put the menu to the side. He gazed out the window as he sipped his coffee. The waitress returned to the table, asking if he'd like a refill while he waited for his lady friend.

"Oh shit, she has been in there for a while. Let me go check on her."

When Savonte' reached the ladies' room, a woman was coming out. He described Janella and asked the lady if she saw her in there.

"Yes, there's only one lady in there who fits that description," the lady replied.

When the lady walked off, Savonte' looked around then went

in. He locked the door behind him to keep anyone else from entering, even though his only purpose for going in was to see if Janella was okay. Janella was sitting on a bench with her head resting in both of her hands. Savonte' approached her with concern. When he squatted down in front of her, she reached out and gripped him around his neck. She felt him relax in her arms and she began to kiss him on his neck. He immediately became putty in her hands. As she slowly began to stand, he stood with her. They stood close as she kissed his lips, face and neck. She glided her hands down his body to his crotch. Slowly, she unbuttoned and unzipped his pants. As his trousers dropped to the floor, she guided him to sit on the bench. As she straddled him, he reached under her dress, pulling her panties to the side. She sat on a firm piece of flesh that expanded and caused her insides to quiver. He embraced her tightly, pressing his face into her breast bone. She then held his face with both of her hands as she sucked his lips. The slow, up and down motion eventually became fast, hard and intense. They both were hot and sweaty, but they hadn't quite reached their peak. Janella put a little more energy into her strokes and Savonte' brought it on home.

"Whew, what brought that on?" Savonte' asked as he wiped sweat from his forehead.

Janella didn't respond. She smiled, winked and got up from his lap. She cleaned up in the sink as best she could in a public restroom, but Savonte' merely zipped his pants, washed his hands and followed her back to the table.

The waitress came over to the table with hot coffee when she saw them return. She stood next to Savonte' and the smell of sex overwhelmed her nostrils. Her nose curled up and she quickly took their order and raced toward the kitchen. Janella and Savonte' chuckled as she raced off, knowing that she knew what they'd just done.

Savonte' was feeling so good he'd forgotten he was upset with Janella. They sipped coffee and chatted while they waited for their food. Janella was high off of the sweet taste of triumph. She inwardly gloated about reeling Savonte' back into her good graces. Their food arrived, they ate and then left to go shopping.

As they reached the furniture store where Janella was dying to buy her furniture, she spotted a full length, mink coat that she couldn't do without. She took Savonte' by the hand, leading him into the store. While Janella tried on a number of jackets and coats, Savonte' sat on the leather sofa in a fog. Savonte's cell phone rang while Janella interacted with the sales clerk. Moments after Savonte' began his phone conversation, he got up off of the sofa and walked toward the front door. During the course of his conversation, he became agitated. To keep from making a scene, he stepped out of the store. The conversation grew into a heated argument. He used a few, strong, choice words, then clicked Evan off of the phone. Obviously steamed, he put his hand in his pocket and returned inside the store. Anger swelled his face and he clinched his jaws tightly as he went back to his spot on the sofa. He tossed his cell phone back and forth from hand to hand, contemplating what to do.

Evan had informed him that he'd just learned that he, Tony and Savonte' had lost several hundred thousand dollars in a deal they'd invested in a few months ago. Savonte' quickly realized that his cash flow, livelihood and life style had been compromised. Janella had finally narrowed her choices down to six different selections.

She came bouncing over to Savonte' for him to help her decide on a chinchilla jacket or a mink coat. The mention of chinchilla made him want to pass out. He was ready to go find several rabbits and stitch a coat for her by hand. Instead, he reached up and checked out the price tag on them both. He raised a brow, trying not to show that as of five minutes ago, he couldn't afford to buy her a loaf of bread without wondering if that was the last thing he would buy. He shrugged his shoulders, indicating he couldn't decide. He needed space to think of a way out without severely embarrassing himself. He didn't have a lot of time to make a rational decision. He reached into his pocket for a stick of gum, when he felt a checkbook. A trigger went off in his mind, reminding him that he had Cynthia's checkbook and bank card. He knew her cash was liquid and could handle whatever the price was for the jacket and the coat.

He sat back, relaxed, confident, knowing that he was saved from embarrassment and humiliation. Moments later, the sales clerk walked passed him, holding a jacket in one hand and a coat in the other. She smiled at him as she proceeded to the register.

Janella joined him on the sofa, kissing him on the cheek as she sat down. Savonte' eased to the edge of the sofa before standing. Of course he didn't want Janella to know that he had to use Cynthia's money, so he patted her on her thigh and told her to sit tight while he took care of business. Janella was happy to sit still. She'd been on her feet since they got there and her feet needed a rest before they went to the furniture store. Savonte' was devastated by the news he'd received from Evan and had completely forgotten about the furniture that Janella wanted. After spending several thousand dollars on the jacket and coat, he wasn't up for anymore shopping.

Janella on the other hand, had no idea that Savonte' had financial issues that he was dealing with. She'd struck out to get furniture and she had no intentions of going home without any. In her mind the furs were an unexpected bonus. When Janella saw the clerk bagging the furs, she got up and went to the desk. She linked her arms into one of Savonte's arms and rested her head on the upper part of his arm. As he looked down, she raised her head and their eyes met. She smiled and whispered; "Thank you".

As they left the store, Savonte' headed in the direction of the car. Janella stopped abruptly and then asked, "What about the furniture store?"

Savonte' turned slowly to respond, but hesitated before speaking. Initially he was going to tell her that he'd spent enough for the day, but decided since he was spending Cynthia's money, it really didn't matter how much he spent. "Oh, I was going to put these in the trunk of the car. They're too heavy to carry around for too long."

"OK," Janella said, as she started walking again.

When they entered the furniture store, Janella pointed herself in the direction of the set she had her heart set on. But before getting to that particular set, she saw a new arrival that was on display. It was a stunning beauty of chiseled wood. She walked back and forth between the two sets, trying to make a decision. Savonte' stood back, watching her move about like a jack rabbit. He didn't give a damn which one she picked since Cynthia's money was paying for it. Janella was so torn between the two bedroom sets she asked Savonte' to help her decide.

"I don't care, they're both nice. Hell, do 'eenie, meenie, minie, mo'," he said, unconcerned.

Fine, motherfucker . . . since you don't care, I'll get a picture and accessories, too.

Janella turned around and started browsing for more to buy. After finding a couple of pictures, a statue and a large, floor standing candle holder, she informed the sales person of what she wanted to purchase, without bothering to consult him. Before they rang up the sale, Janella pointed to Savonte' for payment. Savonte' joined Janella at the counter, but asked her to go have a seat. Naturally, he still didn't want her to know that he wasn't spending his own money. After the transaction was complete, Savonte' motioned for Janella. She had to set up the delivery time, because Savonte' wasn't about to sit and wait for the delivery people to show.

Savonte' was deep in thought and feeling slightly guilty about spending Cynthia's money, but Janella had shopped up an appetite. She convinced him to take her to lunch. He mumbled under his breath, but agreed just the same.

All the while they were in the restaurant there was no conversation. Savonte' was not good company, so Janella gave him his space. She had no intentions of getting dragged into his shit. She was not interested in taking on his problems. She could have cared less about his troubles. As long as he could buy for her and take care of business in the bedroom, she was content.

Savonte' didn't order anything to eat, but it didn't stop Janella from devouring everything on her plate. Savonte' was ready to take her home so that he could deal with his financial situation. He couldn't understand how things could be so fucked up. What he did know was that if Evan or Tony caused the catastrophe, he was going to kill them both, or have them killed.

He drove Janella home, but didn't get out when they pulled into the driveway. Janella didn't want to be bothered anyway, so she leaned over and kissed him on the cheek. She exited the car and walked to the back to remove her coats from the trunk, after which Savonte' drove off.

CHAPTER TWELVE

12

Back at Ardelia's, she and Cynthia anxiously await the

release of the accident report as they discuss the 'what if's' regarding Blade. Cynthia wasn't convinced that Blade was the dead man that Ardelia overheard the men talking about, but Ardelia was leaning toward her gut feeling. With every part of her being, Ardelia felt there was a connection. If she was wrong, she'd have to start from scratch to find out who Savonte' really was and what his intentions were with Cynthia. From the very first moment Ardelia met Savonte', he wreaked of bullshit. Getting her friend free from his unsavory clutches had become her personal mission.

Although Cynthia had finally jumped on board with Ardelia, Cynthia still didn't want to face the fact that she'd been had. She was really having difficulty accepting that she'd let another asshole like Thomas into her life. She was weak for handsome, powerful men, but Thomas and Savonte' took their looks and business acumen to a whole other level. All Cynthia needed was for Savonte' to leave a trail of dead bodies behind like Thomas did. If Ardelia was right, there was at least one.

The more Cynthia thought about the possibility of Savonte' using her, the more she digressed into the hell hole she'd fallen into with Thomas a short time ago. After struggling her way through years of an abusive marriage, the murders of friends and the overwhelming deception Thomas inflicted on her life, Cynthia was determined not to allow Savonte' to destroy her. If he turned out to be as dangerous as Ardelia believed he was, she needed to find out about him now.

Cynthia and Ardelia remained in their neutral space, but were thinking about the same thing. The minutes turned into hours and eventually the hours turned daylight into night.

Savonte' was at home on the phone ripping into Evan and Tony about the financial hit they'd taken. He demanded an explanation as to how they had been blind sided. Neither of them offered a solid explanation. Evan told him to stop acting like a bitch. Evan tried to make Savonte' understand that they all suffered the same, but Savonte' wasn't hearing him. All Savonte' knew was that he had grown accustomed to a lavish lifestyle and he wasn't willing to give it up. He would do whatever he had to in order to maintain his status. While they were on the line, Tony had another call click in. When he returned he said, "Hey guys, I've got to go. Janella is on the other line and she wants to talk. I haven't talked to her since we met and I'm dying to talk to her."

I just spent thousands of dollars on that bitch today, and she's calling

Tony??!! What the fuck is going on?" Savonte' thought angrily. No one responded to Tony so he hung up. Evan remained on the phone with Savonte', but he wasn't able to calm him down.

Tony paced the floor while talking to Janella, as he was too hyped to sit still. After a while, he relaxed on the sofa. He became a bit more relaxed than he realized. He held the cordless phone with the side of his face, as it rested on his shoulder. He propped one hand behind his head and the other inside of his pants on his genitals.

He listened to Janella go on and on about her new furs and furniture. She neglected to disclose that Savonte' had bought them though. She made a comment or two that Tony would have to come over and try out the new mattress, and Tony was more than willing.

He began daydreaming about being with her. He envisioned her long legs wrapped around his body, which caused feelings to stir in him as if she was pressed against him. Janella knew exactly what was going on so she added fuel to the fire. She had him worked up into a lather. Boy was she good at luring men with her feminine wiles. Abruptly, she found a reason to get off the phone and left him to get his rocks off all by himself. He was yearning to be with her, but this would do for the moment.

He lay there wearing a smile that lit up the room. He fantasized about what he would do to her on her new mattress. Janella hadn't given him a second thought. She moved on to the next one. She called Savonte' to chit chat, but he was as cold as ice. He gritted his teeth and bit his bottom lip to keep cool.

Tony had told Savonte' and Evan that Janella was on the other line, but he hadn't told Janella that he was talking to Savonte'. Janella had no idea why Savonte' was being so cold, but she didn't waste any time trying to figure it out. Hell, she had two new furs and new furniture to keep her comfortable. She turned her thoughts to her estranged husband whom she was longing to be with. After ending the call with Savonte', she picked up the phone to call him.

Janella repeatedly asked her husband when they would be together again, but he continually told her 'soon.' She didn't like being away from him, but he had forced her to establish a new life without him. She hung on the phone until there was nothing more to say.

She was feeling guilty about sleeping around and using these men for financial gain, but she didn't feel as though she had any other choice. Her options were slim since her husband had more important things to do.

Janella was anxious for her new furniture to arrive, Tony was looking forward to seeing her, Savonte' couldn't wait to find out what happened to his money and Cynthia and Ardelia were biting their nails, waiting for the accident report.

CHAPTER THIRTEEN

13

D ays passed and Ardelia couldn't stand to wait any

longer to see if the accident report had arrived at Cynthia's house. She got dressed and let Cynthia know that she was going to her house to check the mail. Cynthia sat on the edge of the bed, smoking cigarettes and anticipating what Ardelia would return with.

When Ardelia pulled up in front of Cynthia's house, she gasped. The front of the house was an unsightly mess. Newspapers were piled up in the yard and the mail was overflowing from the mailbox. Her first thought was, *Why the fuck hasn't Savonte' been over to pick this shit up?* She got out of her car, slammed the door and commenced to pick up wet, soggy newspapers from the yard. She stacked them in a pile near the garage door. She retrieved the mail from the mailbox and slung it into her car. She then pulled her car closer to the house, but didn't get out. She glanced over into Frank's yard and noticed that his newspapers were scattered about his yard, too. She wondered why Frank hadn't picked up Cynthia's mail and papers, but apparently, he hadn't been around himself. It was possible that Frank was out of town so Ardelia didn't ponder over it for long, because it wasn't Frank's job to see to the house and mail, it was Savonte's.

She picked up all the mail that she'd thrown into the seat and sifted through it looking for an envelope from the police department. As luck would have it, that particular envelope was the last one in the stack. She was so excited about receiving it that she didn't bother to go into the house. She couldn't get back to her house fast enough.

When she got back to the house, Cynthia was still perched on the edge of the bed smoking cigarettes. Cynthia was reaching for the envelope as soon as Ardelia stepped into the room. She ripped the envelope open, scanning the report for the name of the person she'd collided with. Ardelia paced back and forth, biting her thumb nail. Cynthia held on to the report for so long, Ardelia couldn't stand the pressure and snatched it out of her hand. She got a glimpse of the name, tossed it on the bed next to Cynthia and ran out the door towards her car. As she ran, she told Cynthia she'd call her from her cell phone. Cynthia remained seated on the side of the bed, reading the report. Cynthia had picked apart every word on the page, but nothing seemed to be out of the ordinary.

Ardelia knew the area of the address on Blade's driver's license. She drove in that direction hoping to find someone home. It was possible that someone could tell her what hospital he'd been transferred to.

By the time Ardelia got to Dover Street, she was excited. She was two blocks away from getting to Blade. When she reached the corner of Whitehaven, she began to turn right, but there was nothing on the block. Whitehaven was vacant as far as she could see. She thought that maybe she'd gotten turned around. She drove up two more blocks to Dayton, then to Hillside. There was no hint of habitation in the area. It was apparent that there was a plan to build on all the land. She'd been in the area two months or so before and all the houses were still standing. She was very puzzled, but more furious that once again she'd reached a dead end to finding Blade. She pulled over to the curb and called Cynthia.

"Cynthia, Blade's house is not here!" Ardelia said frantically.

"What do you mean his house isn't there?"

"His house and every house for blocks has been condemned."

"Awe shit. We're right back where we started."

"I'll be back shortly and we can figure out what to do."

It was driving Ardelia nuts that she kept coming up short in her quest to find Blade. On the drive back home she found herself stopped at a traffic light next to Savonte'. She'd glanced over at him, but he hadn't seen her. When the light changed to green, she changed lanes to tail him.

They traveled nearly twelve blocks before Savonte' made a turn. Ardelia hung back a little to keep him from noticing her. A few blocks down, Savonte' turned into a driveway. Ardelia pulled over to the curb a few houses past the house where he turned into the driveway.   She watched him from the rearview mirror as he approached the house. Once he was inside, Ardelia backed up and stopped directly in front of the house. The name on the mailbox read "Dix". *Ah, so this is Blade's house. Bruce Dix, alias Blade has a family, huh?* Ardelia thought.

Ardelia didn't want to sit too long for fear she'd be noticed by Savonte'. She put her car in gear and proceeded to her house. Her mind was spinning with curiosity. Nothing would please her more than to get the dirt on Savonte' and Blade. Her instincts rang danger, loud and clear.

The ride home seemed to take an exceptionally long time, but finally she was there. She ran into the house, huffing and puffing with every step.

"Cynthia! Girl, I found Blade's house!" Ardelia's voice echoed through the house.

Cynthia had made her way from the bedroom to the family room and was sitting on the sofa when Ardelia entered the room. "What did you say?"

"On the way home I saw Savonte' and I followed him. He..."

"Followed him? Why would you follow him?" Cynthia interjected.

"Damn, would you let me finish?"

Cynthia sat in anticipation, while Ardelia collected her thoughts. Ardelia took a deep breath and then continued.

"When I saw Savonte', something within me made me think

he could lead me to Blade. I'm glad I followed my instincts, because he went straight to Blade's house. I didn't see Blade, but the name on the mailbox was Dix, which is Blade's last name. A woman answered the door and I assume it was Blade's wife."

"So now what?"

"Hell, I don't know. Let me think for a second."

They both sat in silence as the wheels turned in their heads. After a while, Cynthia blurted out her assessment of the dilemma.

"We don't really know what we're looking for, so getting answers without a real question is next to impossible," Cynthia commented.

"We know something's not right, so what do you propose we do?"

Cynthia didn't have an answer to that question, so they continued to sit and think. They both were at a loss for words until, out of the blue, Ardelia had concocted a plan.

"Okay, okay, this is what we'll do," Ardelia said excitedly, while bouncing up and down on the sofa. "Since I have the address, we can get the telephone number from the Internet. I can call and pretend to be from Memorial. I can say that I have some personal belongings that Blade left in his room and I'd like to have them sent to the facility where he was transferred. This way we'll know where he is. I can go there and talk to him."

"What's the back up plan if the wife won't tell you where he is?"

"Damn, Cynthia, think positive."

"I'm just thinking ahead, just in case."

"Then think ahead and come up with 'Plan B', you know...just in case." Ardelia said as she moved toward the computer.

Ardelia searched the Internet for the telephone number, while Cynthia put her brain to work on a backup plan. Ardelia found the number and immediately picked up the telephone. She dialed slowly, while preparing her speech. On the second ring, a soft, timid voice answered, "Hello."

"Hi. I'm calling from Memorial. I need to know the facility where Mr. Dix was transferred. He left some personal items in his room and I want to send them to him. His chart has already been sent and I don't remember the name of the facility. Can you help me out?" Ardelia spoke swiftly.

"Oh sure, he's at Our Lady of Lords Rehabilitation Center in Arlington Heights."

"Thanks," Ardelia offered, as she quickly disconnected the call. She smiled at Cynthia as she turned back to the computer. Almost instantly Ardelia obtained the address and telephone number for Our Lady of Lords in Arlington Heights. She and Cynthia put their heads together and came up with a precise script to follow. Since Blade had already met Ardelia, he would be guarded and unresponsive to her. Therefore, she had to have her act together if she expected to get anywhere with him. Cynthia hobbled behind Ardelia as she headed to the kitchen to fix something to eat.

"So, Ardelia, who is the dead man? We know it's not Blade now."

"I don't know. Maybe Blade had something to do with it. It would be too coincidental if the dead man had something to do with Savonte' or Blade."

Meanwhile, at Blade's house, Savonte' was furious with Sinclair, Blade's wife, for giving out information to an unknown person over the phone. Sinclair was oblivious to Savonte's unscrupulous lifestyle and until he started raking her over the coals, she had no idea that this good looking, well spoken, well dressed, polished business man was a slithering snake. The look in his eyes and his venomous tone caused her to fear him. She too now had questions for Blade, and she wanted Savonte' to leave her house. She was too afraid to ask him to leave, so she mentioned how tired she was and that she wanted to take a nap. Savonte' knew she was trying to get rid of him, so he left.

Savonte' headed for the treatment center, while Sinclair called Blade. As soon as Blade answered the phone Sinclair lit into him, demanding answers. Blade tried to calm her, but his meek, timid, wife was out of control. She was afraid that her family was in danger and she needed for Blade to come clean so that she would know how to handle this situation. However, Blade wouldn't budge. He knew how resourceful Savonte' was so he wouldn't talk much on the phone. He gained control of the conversation and convinced Sinclair that there was nothing to worry about. He asked her to come see him and she agreed to see him the next day. Sinclair had a burning desire to talk to the lady who'd called from Memorial, but didn't know her name.   She moped around the rest of the evening, anticipating the next day.

By now, Savonte' had made it to the center and Ardelia was on her way as well.   Savonte' gave Blade the third degree, and instructed him not to talk to anyone about their business dealings. He emphasized that Blade should not tell Sinclair anything. He knew that Sinclair would tell everything she knew, with the slightest bit of pressure. He motioned to Blade for him to zip his lips, as he left the room.

Ardelia pulled into the parking lot, but remained in her car. She noticed Savonte's vehicle, so she parked a few cars behind his and waited for him to come out. She didn't know how long he'd been there, but she wasn't leaving until she'd seen Blade. Not long after she got comfortable, she saw Savonte' approaching his car. She watched and waited for him to pull off before getting out of her car. By the time she made it to the door, a security guard was locking it. She asked him to open the door, but he pointed to the visiting hours sign and walked away. Ardelia's shoulders slouched and her head bowed as she slowly turned to go back to her car.

Damn it. If I hadn't waited for the asshole to come out, I would have made it inside, Ardelia thought in frustration.

She started her car and began her journey home.

Cynthia was patiently waiting to find out what Ardelia had

learned. When she heard the front door open she became anxious. Ardelia entered the room, deflated from temporary defeat.

"What happened?" Cynthia asked with excitement. Ardelia shook her head in disgust before answering.

"I didn't find out anything. Savonte' was there when I arrived, so I had to wait for him to leave. By the time I got to the front door visiting hours were over and security was locking up for the night."

"That's all right. There's always tomorrow."

"Yeah, but we've continually run into road blocks. With every step forward, something happens to put us two steps back."

Cynthia was disappointed and Ardelia was disgusted with the lack of answers due to all the unexpected events. They went to their bedrooms to retire for the night.

The night passed quickly and the next day Ardelia and Sinclair must have awakened at the same time and followed the exact same routines. They arrived at the rehabilitation center at the same time, literally walking though the front door together. Neither knew who the other one was. Sinclair wished all night that she'd gotten the name of the woman who'd called from Memorial. She didn't realize her wish had come true and the woman was right next to her.

As they proceeded down the hallway, Ardelia began to lag behind Sinclair by a few steps. Sinclair knew exactly where she was going, but since Ardelia didn't know where Blade's room was, she looked at the name plates posted outside of every room. By the time she reached Bruce Dix's room, Sinclair was nowhere in sight.

Ardelia was so focused on finding the room, she'd completely forgotten about the woman she'd walked in with. As she stood outside of Blade's room she hesitated, speculating on the outcome. She could see Blade lying in the bed and she was glad to see he was alone. As she proceeded into the room, Sinclair came out of the bathroom. Neither was expecting to see the other, so needless to say, they were shocked.

Ardelia had a very distinctive voice, once heard, there was and immediate association. Neither of them knew what to say, but Ardelia was the most uncomfortable, so she felt compelled to say something. The moment she spoke, Sinclair's eyes bulged and her mouth dropped open. Ardelia didn't realize Sinclair had recognized her voice, but she knew something had Sinclair spooked. Sinclair's reaction made Ardelia a little shaky, but how Ardelia felt was nothing compared to what was going through Blade's mind. He sensed his wife's mood and realized that Ardelia's presence only meant more questions and trouble. He wanted to disappear under the covers, but instead, Sinclair struck up a light conversation with Ardelia, as she politely ushered her into the hallway.

Sinclair admitted to Ardelia that she recognized her voice from the phone call, and she also let it be known that she was uneasy about Savonte' and whatever he had Bruce mixed up in. She told Ardelia to go ahead and leave and that she would get as many answers from Bruce as she could. They exchanged numbers and agreed to meet for lunch.

Sinclair returned to the room with Bruce, but before he could ask any questions, Sinclair started drilling him with questions. He went against the instructions Savonte' had given him and told his wife everything. Blade not only trusted Sinclair to keep what he'd told her in confidence, but if she were put in danger she needed to know what she was dealing with. She spent several hours with him before leaving to meet Ardelia. Although Bruce had come clean with everything, Sinclair didn't tell him that she was meeting Ardelia. In Sinclair's mind, she was protecting him and she would move heaven and hell for him. Sinclair left Blade in good spirits as she left for the restaurant to meet Ardelia.

Ardelia told Sinclair bits and pieces of her suspicions and she managed to get Sinclair on her bandwagon. They decided to meet at Cynthia's to map out a plan. They finished their meal and left.

CHAPTER FOURTEEN

14

C ynthia was a little skittish about the unknown woman

Ardelia had brought home. She was even more guarded once she found out who she was. Cynthia observed Sinclair's body language while Sinclair and Ardelia talked. Cynthia slowly loosened up as she recognized Sinclair's determination to find out what Savonte' was up to. It was clear they were on the same page, so Cynthia joined in the discussion.

Cynthia was so comfortable she mentioned the conversation Ardelia had overheard about the dead man and the mention of Blade's name. She didn't know that Ardelia had held back information from Sinclair. Ardelia shot a look towards Cynthia in an effort to stifle her, but Sinclair was all over it. Actually, it was a good thing. Sinclair had all the answers to that particular incident. She told them the man's name was Frank and he lived on Pine Street. She went on to say, "He got into an altercation with Savonte', so Savonte' had his men kill him. Frank had found out something about Savonte' and threatened to go to the police. He mentioned something about a woman, but I can't remember her name."

Ardelia turned to Cynthia, and Cynthia was already looking Ardelia's way. They said simultaneously, "Frank? On Pine Street?!"

"Oh my God! So that's why when I went to your house the other day Frank's newspapers were scattered in the yard," Ardelia said nervously.

"You didn't tell me that," Cynthia responded.

"I figured he was out of town and I didn't give it another thought."

Cynthia covered her face with her hands and silently cried. When she raised her head, she wiped the tears across her face in an effort to erase the pain. She swallowed hard, took a deep breath and they talked more about the situation. As their stories intertwined, the pieces all started to fit. The two men Ardelia described were guys that had been around Savonte' for years, according to Sinclair. They looked like they were hit men, but Sinclair never had a reason to think they really were.

After fitting all of the pieces together, Sinclair was a little apprehensive about going home. Cynthia convinced Sinclair to keep a normal routine so that no one got suspicious. Sinclair agreed, but she was scared shitless. Sinclair left for home to dig through Bruce's paperwork to see what she could find out. Cynthia and Ardelia decided to call it a night so they'd be ready for their adventure the next day. Cynthia wasn't supposed to leave the house unless she was going to therapy, but there was no way she was going to let Ardelia go it alone. Since Chris was visiting with a friend, they didn't have to worry about her asking any questions. The last thing they needed was for Chris to stumble into the mess they were uncovering.

Neither Ardelia nor Cynthia could sleep. Ardelia wanted to leave in the middle of the night to go to Cynthia's house, but she didn't want to leave Cynthia alone. Plus, she wasn't too comfortable going there at night alone, especially, now that Frank had turned up dead. They continued to toss and turn.

On the other side of town, Sinclair hadn't given sleep a thought. She was in Bruce's home office, digging through drawers and files. At three a.m. she came across a copy of a check written to Mr. Bruce Dix. The name on the check was different than the signature. Immediately, Sinclair felt sick to her stomach, recalling that the pre-printed name on the check was the same name she'd heard Savonte' mention when she heard him talking about Frank. Without hesitation, she picked up the phone and called Ardelia.

Since Cynthia and Ardelia were still very much awake, they both picked up the phone when it rang. Sinclair stumbled and stammered over her words from the other end of the phone. Cynthia was able to calm her enough to get her to speak calmly.

"Okay, okay," Sinclair whispered. She took a deep breath and proceeded to tell them what she'd found.

"I just found a check written to my husband in the amount of twenty-five thousand dollars!"

"That's not unusual for investigative services, is it?" Ardelia asked.

"No, not really, but let me finish. The check is signed by Savonte' Black, but the name printed on the check isn't Savonte's."

A lump hit the pit of Cynthia's stomach and a knot seemed to cut off the air path in her throat. At that very moment, she knew what Sinclair was about to say.

"The check belongs to Cynthia Evans." For a few moments they all were silent, until they heard Cynthia sniffle. She laid the phone down next to her on the bed and let out a horrific scream. Ardelia jumped to her feet, threw the phone onto the bed and raced downstairs to her side.

Sinclair held the phone, shaking with fear, while waiting for one of them to return to the line. When Ardelia returned to the line, she told Sinclair to get out of the house and bring what she'd found over to them.

Sinclair put everything back in place, with the exception of what she was taking with her. She grabbed it and headed for the door. She turned the doorknob and swung the door open. To her surprise Savonte' was standing in the doorway. Sinclair was terrified at the sight of him, but she tried to appear at ease. Savonte' asked, "Where are you going this time of morning?"

Sinclair put the ball back in his court and asked, "What are you doing here this time of the morning?"

"I came to check on you since I was so hard on you when I

was here last."

"You wanted to check on me in the wee hours of the morning? Come on, Savonte'. What's really up?"

"No, really, I only came to the door because I saw the light on."

"Well, I'm on my way out."

"I can see that. Where are you going?"

"My husband is in the rehab center. I don't have to answer to anyone else." Sinclair barked, but realized from the look on his face that she'd come on a little too strong.

Savonte' raised a brow and bit the side of his bottom lip. He stepped to the side and allowed her to step out of the house. Sinclair rushed down the steps and got into her car. Savonte' stood on the porch as she drove away. Savonte' was very uneasy with Sinclair's behavior and was seriously concerned with what she might know. He flipped open his cell phone and called his hit men. They conversed for a bit, then he got into his car and left.

When Sinclair arrived at Ardelia's house, Ardelia was watching for her through the window. Sinclair rushed into the house and quickly closed the door behind her. She was short of breath from running and panic. Before Cynthia or Ardelia could ask anything, Sinclair explained what she'd found and told them about Savonte' showing up at her door.

"This thing is much bigger than we expected. We are way over our heads and I'm scared."

While Sinclair was talking, Cynthia was looking through the papers Sinclair had brought. All of a sudden Cynthia gasped, covered her mouth and started crying again.

"What did you find, Cynthia?" Ardelia asked. Cynthia tossed the papers into Ardelia's lap and crossed her arms, awaiting Ardelia's reaction. Since Sinclair didn't really know Cynthia or Ardelia, she didn't know all of the players. Sinclair had no idea that Cynthia was a partner in an architectural firm or about the tragedies she had experienced. Ardelia read through all the papers, but the last page took Ardelia by surprise, too. The spreadsheet contained money transfers from Robinson, Cavil, Lee and Evans. They laid all the papers onto the dining room table to determine where they should start. They needed to go to the bank, to Cynthia's house and to the firm. Since it was Sunday, they couldn't go to the bank, but it was perfect for going to the office. Cynthia and Ardelia threw on comfortable clothes and they all left for Cynthia's office.

On the way there, their heads buzzed with questions. Cynthia was dying to know who in the firm was connected to Savonte' and Blade. It came to Cynthia that this was the reason why Maurice believed she was embezzling money. Either he was the culprit or whoever was cooking the books had really done a good job of making it look as though she had really embezzled money from the firm.

When they got inside the office building, Cynthia led the way to Paulie's office. She hobbled to the door, using her key to get in. They ransacked her office, but to no avail. They put everything back into place then proceeded to Billie's office. Once again, they went through every drawer and file cabinet, but still no evidence. Inside Maurice's office, Ardelia searched the drawers, Sinclair searched the cherry wood file cabinets, and Cynthia looked through the pile of papers on his desk. Ardelia and Sinclair came up with nothing, but Cynthia got her hands on all the paperwork Maurice had used when he confronted her with embezzlement allegations. She handed the papers to Ardelia and asked her to make copies. Cynthia couldn't find the strength to stand; her head became cloudy, her legs felt numb, and her stomach was on fire. Sinclair stood in the middle of the floor and watched Cynthia silently shed tears.

When Ardelia returned with the copies, Cynthia put the original papers back where she'd found them. However, the copies didn't exactly tell them much more than they already knew. They needed to luck up on who was responsible and why they were so determined to bring Cynthia down.

They decided to go into Cynthia's office, but as they passed Marge's desk, Cynthia got a glimpse of the top portion of a spreadsheet. As she pulled the paper from the middle of the stack, she rhetorically asked, "What the hell would Marge be doing with this spreadsheet? Her duties don't consist of preparing or updating spreadsheets." Before she could get the words completely out of her mouth, she dropped the paper as if it were hot. Sinclair reached over and picked it up. When Sinclair gasped, Ardelia snatched the paper out of Sinclair's hand.

"Well I'll be damned. This is the original to the spreadsheet you found in Blade's office!" Ardelia shouted.

"The more we dig, the more twisted it gets," Sinclair added.

"But what could Marge have to do with all of this?" Cynthia asked.

"Maybe it's one of the partners and they had her make copies or mail them or something. That old lady doesn't have the savvy to plan anyone's demise. Throw her out of your mind. Let's keep digging and see what else we can find," Ardelia commanded.

"Fine. Let's get out of here in case one of the partners happens to show up and catch us here. Hell, from the looks of it, they want to convict me and get me out of the firm anyway. I don't want to see either of them until I have evidence to prove my innocence. Let's go to my house," Cynthia suggested.

On the ride to Cynthia's, they were all closemouthed, as they each struggled to make sense of it all. As they rounded the corner to Cynthia's house, Ardelia tried to prepare Cynthia for the unsightliness of the front of the house. After Ardelia's last visit, she was sure that the grass was taller, the weeds had grown and more papers would be scattered about the yard, not to mention that Frank's yard was an unsightly mess, too. Between the two houses the lack of care had surely decreased the property value. However, the lack of habitability displayed from the outside paled in comparison to what they found when they got inside.

Ardelia had already opened the door by the time Cynthia

made her way to the porch. Ardelia and Sinclair stood in the foyer, unable to move by what they saw. When Cynthia stepped across the threshold, she began to hyperventilate. She bent over, resting her weight on her crutch. "NO...NO...NO! This cannot be happening!" Cynthia yelled at the top of her lungs. "Why would someone break into my house and turn my things topsy turvy?"

Ardelia and Sinclair took a few steps closer to console Cynthia, but angry and confused, Cynthia pushed them away. She was in no mood to be pampered and babied.

"I'm going to call the police," Ardelia said. When she picked up the phone, there was no dial tone. She extended the receiver out in front of her and looked at it as if the receiver could speak. "What's wrong?" Cynthia asked.

"There's no dial tone."

"This is really some weird shit. What the hell am I tangled up in?" Sinclair snapped.

Cynthia and Ardelia gave Sinclair a cold, 'bitch, don't go there' look, then turned away from her without responding. Sinclair realized that she'd said the wrong thing, so she tried to recover from it.

"I'm sorry. I'm in this with you since my husband apparently is involved somehow. I'm just scared. This is not something I've ever had to deal with and it just keeps getting worse."

Ardelia pulled out her cell phone and called the police. While they waited for the police to arrive, Ardelia wandered around to see what the rest of the downstairs looked like. She wasn't about to go upstairs until the police got there. Sinclair stayed near the door with Cynthia, in case they needed to get out quickly. Ardelia shouted from the kitchen, "The electricity is off, too!"

She swiftly walked back into the foyer with Cynthia and Sinclair. They were all feeling a little squeamish, so they decided to wait for the police outside.

Two police cars pulled into the driveway shortly after they went outside. The first two officers went inside to check out the house. The other two officers stopped to talk to the Cynthia, Ardelia and Sinclair. Ardelia had a funny look on her face as the two officers started talking to them. Ardelia recognized their voices, but couldn't quite recall from where. Cynthia stared for a moment too, then it came to her.

"Hey, you're the two cops who helped us one night downtown. Do you remember us?"

The officers looked at each other as one of them responded, "Sorry, we see and help so many people it's hard to pinpoint one incident.

"Yeah, I knew I recalled your voices, but I couldn't remember from where. But you didn't have on uniforms that night, so you must have been off duty, huh?" Ardelia offered.

The second cop spoke up remarking, "If we didn't have on the uniform we had to be off duty."

"Well, we sure are glad you were there that night, off duty or not. Thanks for saving us," Ardelia said.

While the conversations were taking place, Sinclair didn't take her eyes off of the two cops. When the two officers that were in the house came out, they let them know that the coast was clear to go back inside. They all went in into the living room, wading through a maze of clutter.

Feeling comfortable with the police, Cynthia started to tell the whole, sordid story of all the events they'd uncovered. As soon as Sinclair realized the path Cynthia was taking, she jumped in, and redirected the conversation. She controlled the conversation, and convinced the officers that they'd be fine. She ushered the four officers to the door and let them out.

Ardelia knew that Sinclair was onto something, even though she didn't know what. She and Cynthia allowed Sinclair to control the situation, but couldn't wait for her to return to the living room. When she returned, she put her index finger over her lips to keep them quiet. She motioned for them to leave, so they locked up and left the house. Once they were in the car, she leaned forward from the back seat and poked her head between Ardelia and Cynthia

"Those two cops that helped you work for Savonte'. I've seen them with him before and they've been to my house with him once or twice.

"Oh, shit. They're the two guys I overheard talking about the dead man. But I didn't realize they were the cops at that time," Ardelia blurted out.

"I would bet you they ransacked my house and killed Frank," Cynthia speculated.

"If they didn't, they surely had something to do with it," Sinclair responded.

Ardelia started her car and got the hell out of the driveway. They opted not to go directly back to Ardelia's, so they went to a restaurant instead. They were seated in a large booth, which was perfect for laying out all the papers. They ordered several appetizers that they shared. While they waited for their food, they put the papers on the table and tried to arrange them in some type of order. If the papers had dates, they were arranged in date order. The papers that didn't have dates were arranged by sequence of events. There were a few papers that they didn't have a clue where they fit and just as they got them organized their food arrived.

Between bites, Ardelia asked Cynthia a number of questions. Ardelia knew that Cynthia couldn't answer her questions, but she was trying to force Cynthia to see that turning her business affairs over to Savonte' had not been a good idea.

"How could your utilities be shut off?" Ardelia queried Cynthia.

"I've been thinking about that since we left the house. I can't come up with a logical reason," Cynthia responded.

"Were all of your bills current before Savonte' took over?"

"Of course."

"Then the utilities weren't shut off for non-payment, they

were deliberately turned off."

"The theory makes sense, but why?" Sinclair questioned.

"Who knows? None of this shit makes sense. I feel like we're in the freakin' 'Twilight Zone' and we're the only ones visiting," Cynthia added.

They finished their food and left for Ardelia's house.

CHAPTER FIFTEEN

15

Cynthia sat on the sofa, while Ardelia and Sinclair

stretched out on the floor in the family room. They were wrestling over what to do.

"Okay, this is what we have so far," Ardelia remarked, as she sat the stack of papers between them.

"We need to divide between us the responsibilities of who will do what. Someone needs to make phone calls, somebody needs to go to the rehab center to see what else Blade might say and someone needs to stalk Savonte' and his boys," Sinclair instructed.

"Sinclair, you need to go to the rehab center. Blade will tell you more than he'll tell us. Marge doesn't know you, so you might be able to fish around and get information from her. Ardelia, since you've gotten good at playing detective, you should keep tabs on Savonte', Evan and Tony and see what you can find out about those two cops. Be careful with them since they are gun carrying cops and hit men. I don't want you to be their next victim. I'll make all the phone calls, since I'm not supposed to be out anyway," Cynthia directed.

Sinclair wasn't comfortable going home alone and she surely didn't want to stay in her house. She asked Ardelia to go home with her to get a few things. She asked Ardelia if she could stay at her house with them until this mess they'd found themselves in blew over. Although Ardelia was glad that Sinclair had jumped in to help them, unlike Cynthia, Ardelia wasn't about to let a stranger stay in her house. She explained to Sinclair that Chris lived in the house and it was probably best for her to stay somewhere else.

"There's a hotel a few blocks away. It's close enough that I could get to you quickly, if necessary," Ardelia suggested to Sinclair.

Sinclair felt insignificant and unappreciated, but she was too afraid to go it alone, so she agreed to stay in the hotel. Ardelia and Sinclair left to go to Sinclair's house. Cynthia stayed on the sofa, sifting through the papers again. She was hoping that she'd overlooked something that would jump out at her. After reviewing the papers again, she laid them on her chest and drifted off to sleep.

While Cynthia slept, Sinclair and Ardelia were on the other side of town, gathering enough of Sinclair's things to keep her from needing to go home for a while. As they were about to pull out of the driveway, they saw Savonte' drive past the house. The mere fact that he was hovering like a vulture caused them a great deal of concern. It was clear that he knew they were onto something, but he didn't know exactly what or how much. He continued on past the house, knowing that they'd seen him creep by. Once again, he called his boys. He ordered them to watch Cynthia, Ardelia and Sinclair. He didn't want to take any more chances that they'd spot him spying on them again. He gave his boys specific instructions to deal with Cynthia, Ardelia and Sinclair and then he headed for Evan's house.

Cynthia was abruptly awakened by a telephone number that her subconscious was recalling in her sleep. She sat up on the sofa, frantically looking over the papers. At the bottom of one of the pages was a telephone number. Unfortunately, when Ardelia made the copies, she unknowingly cut off the bottom portion of the page. The copy showed only the tops of some numbers, in telephone number format.

Cynthia sat for a few moments, bewildered that every time they got a lead, something managed to set them back. She was starting to feel that it wasn't worth the trouble. She wondered if she should just suck it up, walk away, and start over with a clean slate. The thought only lasted for a few seconds. She got up from the sofa and made her way to the computer. She began to search the phone directory on the Internet. She used every combination possible, trying to match the combination of numbers to a name that she might know. After about twenty different searches she became more frustrated.

Her frustration made her more determined to find out who the number belonged to. She continued to search. The pecking and pounding on the keyboard caused the computer to freeze. She waited and waited for the results to show up on the screen, but the computer was locked up. Deciding to step away to calm her nerves, she turned to get up from the chair, but at that moment, the results popped up on the screen. She began to pant and struggle to breathe, startled by the name and address that was displayed. Before she could come unglued and completely melt down, Ardelia and Sinclair came through the front door. By the time they got into the family room Cynthia was drowning in her tears.

Ardelia walked over near Cynthia, prompting her to point to the computer screen. Sinclair stood in the middle of the floor waiting for one of them to include her in on what was going on.

"I knew that bitch was dirty! I never got the chance to spend more time with her, but I knew the night I introduced her to Savonte', Evan and Tony, that something didn't seem right, the frumpy, polyester, sensible shoe wearing cow," Cynthia blurted out.

"Who are you guys talking about?" Sinclair asked.

"Catherine, Catherine Garrett, one of Cynthia's business associates," Ardelia replied.

"But, I can't figure where she plays into all of this. What does she have in common with all the other players involved?" Ardelia added.

Cynthia couldn't seem to talk. Her tongue felt too heavy to lift and her thoughts were very scattered. She couldn't have said anything that would have made any sense, anyway. Ardelia printed the page and added it to the stack of papers.

Cynthia stared into space, lost in her thoughts. Ardelia had a look of frustration and Sinclair was dumbfounded. The whole ordeal was mystifying, but even though they wouldn't admit it, a small part of them was enjoying the adventure. Unfortunately, they didn't know what was waiting ahead.

Cynthia exited the room, slowly making her way to her bedroom. She closed off the French doors that separated the two rooms and lay across the bed. Ardelia shrugged her shoulders and told Sinclair she would take her back to the hotel.

Within minutes, Ardelia had dropped Sinclair off and returned home. She went into Cynthia's room and lay across the bottom of the bed. As she lay there, she noticed a light outside that quickly flashed on, then off. She raised her head and rested her weight on her elbows. While she waited to see the light flash again, Cynthia became curious.

"What are you looking at, Ardelia?"

"I saw a light flash on and off outside. I'm waiting to see if it flashes again."

"You know, I saw a light flash while you were gone, but I didn't think anything of it."

Ardelia got up and proceeded to turn all the lights out in the house. Her house sat in a cul-de-sac, and, since the house was on the corner, she could see the cars on the cross street. She returned to Cynthia's room and went to the window to see if she could spot anything unusual going on. She saw a black Yukon with dark tinted windows. The Yukon sparkled and glistened against the streetlight.

As Ardelia walked away from the window she commented, "I don't think that any of my neighbors have a vehicle like that. If it sits too long, I'm going to call the police."

"And tell 'em what? A car is parked on the street?" Cynthia remarked jokingly.

Ardelia had to laugh herself.

They sat in the bed with their backs against the headboard, in the dark, in silence. The minutes ticked slowly as they watched the clock change from minute to minute.

"We are really paranoid," Ardelia whispered.

"Why are you whispering?" Cynthia asked.

"I don't know, why, did you?" Ardelia responded.

They burst into laughter as the felt pretty silly about their paranoia. Feeling relieved, Cynthia clicked on the television and Ardelia slid out of the bed as Cynthia pulled the covers up over herself. They both retired for the night.

As Cynthia, Ardelia and Sinclair slept, Janella was on the prowl. Although her new furniture hadn't arrived, she called Tony and asked him to come over. It wasn't clear why she'd reached out to Tony. She seemed to be bed hopping with no purpose. However, Tony had no idea what he was in for.

A short time later, Tony was knocking at Janella's door. Casual conversation and foreplay wasn't on Janella's agenda. She commenced to getting Tony in the mood as soon as he walked through the door. Hours passed quickly as they pleasured each other.

It was difficult for Janella to keep up the act, so she began to power down.   Tony was still fully charged, but Janella's lack of responsiveness forced him to back off. After recognizing that she'd wounded his ego, she snuggled up next to him. Her purpose for inviting him into her bed was to gain information about his partnership with Savonte', Evan and Cynthia. If she didn't stroke his ego, she knew she wouldn't find out anything. She was tired of having sex at that moment, but she gave him a most relaxing massage. Tony relaxed into a state of euphoria as she lay next to him, subtly asking questions. She was clever enough to get what she needed without tipping her hand.

Since Tony has been in partnership with Evan and Savonte' since they established the business, he knew everything about every deal. She got enough information for the time being, and decided to wait to get more at a later time. She kept him close, curling up next to his   naked   body   as   they   drifted   off   to   sleep.

CHAPTER SIXTEEN

16

T he next day seemed to come too soon for Cynthia and

Ardelia. The shiny, black Yukon was still sitting on the side of the house. The suspense was killing them so Ardelia decided to be bold and go outside to check it out. She walked around the truck to see if she could see inside. Lucky for her, the person inside had left the passenger side window cracked. She tiptoed up to get a glance inside. The man inside was sound asleep, but she got a good look at him. She eased down from the window and took off running back into the house. She slammed and locked the door behind her and ran screaming into Cynthia's bedroom.

"Girl, we weren't paranoid last night! There's a man in that Yukon!"

"Who is it?" Cynthia asked as she sat up to light a cigarette.

"It's um, it's...it's one of those cops, one of Savonte's goons, the one named Calvin."

"What?! What the hell is Savonte' up to? I need to get to the bank. Get dressed," Cynthia commanded.

"You have therapy today. They'll be picking you up in two hours. Why don't I ride with you to therapy and we ask the driver to stop at the bank on the way back? This way, hopefully, the cop won't follow the med van. From where he's parked I could get in without him seeing me. He'll be watching an empty house."

"All right, okay, that sounds like a plan."
Cynthia sat on her bed watching the Yukon while Ardelia went to the kitchen to fix them something to eat.

Not long after they ate and dressed, the van pulled up. The driver agreed to let Ardelia ride with them. She watched through the side view mirror to see if the Yukon would follow them, but all the way there, there was no sign of it. During the therapy session, Ardelia contemplated what they'd find out at the bank. After the session ended, the driver drove them to the bank. Once inside, Cynthia looked for an available bank officer. She wanted to sit in an office and discuss her business. She did not want to discuss her financial affairs with a teller. She asked the officer to pull up her accounts and let her see the balances and any activity. The bank officer pulled up her accounts and pointed to the balances.

As he slid the printed copies across the desk to her, he had a serene look on his face. He waited for her reaction as he sat back in his chair.

"What the fuck is this shit? There has to be a mistake!" Cynthia shouted.

As the officer began to respond, Ardelia took the papers from Cynthia's hand.

"Ms. Evans, there doesn't appear to be any errors. What seems to be the problem?"

"What seems to be the problem? Between my two accounts, I only have three thousand dollars! Where the hell is all of my money?"

"As I look at the accounts, I see valid check withdrawals. There's a signed affidavit that gave authorization to a Mr. Savonte' Black. All of the checks written have been signed by him," the officer remarked calmly.

As Cynthia started to shake, Ardelia stepped in. "Just withdraw what's left and we'll have to go home and figure it out."

"Is everything OK, Ms. Evans?" the officer asked, confident that the bank was not liable. As they got up to leave the office, Cynthia caught a glimpse of a man leaving the bank that resembled Savonte'. By the time they got to the teller window, the three thousand dollars had been withdrawn. The man who'd just left was Savonte' and he'd just wiped out both accounts, while she sat in the office, a few feet away.

Cynthia started to lose consciousness and then she collapsed to the floor. Ardelia ran outside to get the therapist from the van. He came in and revived her with smelling salts. When she came to, she told the bank officer that she would take the rest of her business from the bank and would never do business with his bank again.

"I thought you already had when you refinanced your house with another company."

"Refinanced my house! What are you talking about?" Cynthia snapped.

"Why don't you go home, and get yourself together? Give me a call tomorrow, and I'll give you all the paperwork."

All the customers and bank personnel had there eyes glued on Cynthia. Ardelia jerked Cynthia by the arm, after noticing everyone staring.

On the way home, Cynthia asked the therapist if she could do therapy everyday. She wanted to get back to her old self as soon as possible. He agreed to pick her up every morning at nine a.m. Ardelia felt that Cynthia was pushing herself too hard, but she understood her motivation.

Cynthia looked out the window all the way home and realized her life spinning out of control, and there didn't seem to be any way to stop it. Ardelia was torn between anger and sympathy. As hard as it was for Ardelia to see her friend in so much pain, she was irritated that Cynthia had been so pigheaded when she tried to caution her about Savonte', but Ardelia kept those feelings to herself. Everyone around Cynthia seemed to be against her, so Ardelia felt she had to stick by Cynthia's side.

Once they were back in the house, Cynthia really let go of her anger. She ranted and raved while she beat her fist into the pillows on the sofa. Ardelia remained calm, knowing that one of them had to stay focused. Cynthia was the one whose life was unraveling, so she had every right to react the way she was.

A short time later, Sinclair called for Ardelia to pick her up. Ardelia told her it wasn't a good time, but Sinclair insisted. Sinclair told her there was something important they needed to talk about, so Ardelia agreed to pick her up.

When Ardelia pulled up in front of the hotel, Sinclair was standing in front, waiting for her. Sinclair jumped in instantly and told Ardelia about a silver Navigator that she noticed from her window. "It was there all night, but when I woke up this morning it was gone."

So much had happened throughout the day that Ardelia had completely forgotten about the black Yukon that had been parked on the side of her house. She looked for it as she rounded the corner to her house, but it was nowhere in sight.

After they got inside the house, Ardelia filled Cynthia in on what Sinclair had told her. Sinclair proceeded to tell them that as she watched the silver Navigator, the man inside opened the door at one point and she was able to see him.

"Don't tell me, it was one of Savonte's boys," Cynthia remarked.

"Yep, it was one of those cops," Sinclair replied.

"Then it had to be Jason, 'cause Calvin was watching us all night," Ardelia said.

Cynthia decided to let Sinclair know what took place at the bank. She was scared to death about the refinancing that the banker told her about. She was afraid that it was another one of Savonte's scams and she wondered if she was about to lose her house.

They sat around talking about everything that was going on, but they were still dumbfounded. Cynthia had a need to relieve her mind of so many unanswered questions, so she grabbed the phone and started dialing. Ardelia and Sinclair looked at each other and wondered who Cynthia was calling.

"You bastard! What the fuck have you done to my life?" Cynthia screamed into the phone. She knew that Savonte' had answered from a speakerphone, but she didn't know or care if he wasn't alone. Janella shot a glance toward Savonte', but she didn't say anything. Savonte' was stunned that Cynthia had pieced enough together to confront him, but he surely couldn't knuckle under and give a weak, pitiful explanation in front of Janella, so he answered defiantly.

"Hey, lady, you can't blame me for all the poor choices you've made in your life. Call me when you can talk to me like you have some sense," Savonte' barked before hanging up on her.

As soon as Tony left Janella's house, she had gone straight to Savonte's place. She had just gotten there when the call came in. The information she had pumped out of Tony made her want to stick closer to Savonte'. She still didn't know that Savonte' was aware that she'd called Tony right after he'd bought her furs and furniture.

Savonte' played it cool for a little bit, but Cynthia had sent his blood boiling, so he asked Janella to leave. As she left, she pretended she was hurt and disappointed. Once Janella got to her car, she grinned from car to ear. Hearing the conversation between Savonte' and Cynthia had made her day. He still thought she didn't know that he'd purchased her furs and furniture with Cynthia's money, but she did. She knew far more than he thought. Actually, she was monitoring him very closely. While he was busy swindling Cynthia and having Cynthia, Ardelia and Sinclair watched, Janella was watching him.

Savonte' was starting to feel the pressure. He was accustomed to sitting pretty financially, and basically doing what he damn well pleased. He picked up the phone and called Tony. He wanted to know if Tony or Evan had figured out what had happened with the failed Real Estate deal. Savonte' was alarmed by Tony's reaction.

"Man, get the fuck out of here with your Hitler tactics. You've shown me that our business and personal relationships mean very little to you. I don't owe you an explanation for a mother fuckin' thing. As a matter of fact, I intend to dissolve my partnership with you," Tony announced.

"Where is all this coming from?"

"You think you can do whatever the hell you want to do to anyone whenever the fuck you feel like it and the world should stand still while you do it! Let me clue you in on something, my brother. I knew you were fucking Janella and I still fucked her last night. We could have both done her without you sneaking around behind my back."

"Hey, man, I wasn't sneaking behind your back. We met by chance and shit just happened. You mean to tell me you're letting a piece of tail come between us?"

"Yeah, and just for the record, you are the only one who got screwed in the deal. Evan's money will show up in his bank account, but you are just shit out of luck. You're not the only motherfucker in town who knows how to play the game. Now take that to the fucking bank, asshole!"

Before Savonte' could respond, there was a dial tone on the line. Savonte' looked at the receiver and pounded his fist on the table. He reeled with anger.

"This has not been my motherfucking day," He said aloud. Across town at the architectural firm, things were heating up. Maurice called a meeting with the other partners to discuss Cynthia's embezzlement. He provided Billie and Paulie with copies of everything he had. He expressed to them that he wasn't on a quest to railroad her out of the business, but in light of all of the evidence, he couldn't, in clear conscious, allow her to stay. Billie and Paulie were in agreement, but Billie wasn't satisfied with only firing her. She wanted to press criminal charges against her.

"That will be bad PR for the firm, and we have too much business on the table that could be jeopardized," Maurice replied.

"So she just walks away Scott free?" Paulie bellowed.

"She won't be too free. She won't get our usual separation package and she will not be paid any more compensation. I already had payroll stop any checks to be paid to her. As much money as she's taken, I'm sure she has it stored away somewhere. She can live off of that, as far as I'm concerned," Maurice said calmly.

"I'm going to make a few calls to some people in the business, so they won't hire the thieving bitch," Billie fumed.

"Be very discreet and very careful how you deliver a message like that. I don't want what you say to come back and bite us in the ass."

They adjourned their meeting and returned to their offices. Paulie called Marge into her office, giving her instructions to have building services pack up Cynthia's office, change the locks and change the password on her voice mail. As Marge was leaving Paulie gave her a couple of more instructions.

"Let me know the password to her voice mail when it's changed and I'll record the greeting. This way, I can have all her business calls redirected to me. As a matter of fact, have all the locks changed, she has keys to everything," Paulie ordered.

When Marge returned to her desk, she made the phone calls Paulie had instructed her to make. She then made a personal call. She whispered into the receiver as she covered it with her hand.

"The partners just fired her. They've stopped her pay and they're changing the locks. I'll keep you posted. I've gotta go, Paulie's calling me. Bye," Marge whispered.

"Yes, Paulie?"

"Place an order to change our stationary, the names on the door and the sign in front of the building. Get her name off of everything," Paulie ordered.

The partners conducted business as usual, as if Cynthia never existed.

As the day wore on Cynthia was still in shock, but Ardelia and Sinclair had decided to get geared up on what they'd planned days ago. Instead of splitting up, they rode together. The first stop was the treatment center. Ardelia stayed in the car while Sinclair went in to talk to Bruce.

Sinclair shared with Bruce all the stuff that had been going on. Since he knew how treacherous Savonte' could be, he was very concerned for his wife. However, there was some additional light that he could shed. He knew that Cynthia had been hand picked. It was no coincidence that she was asked to be a partner in the real estate deals. He also told her that there was an ex-partner, who hangs out at Syncopations. He told her to go talk to Cleofus Aiken at the club.

"How will I know who he is?" Sinclair asked.

"He goes by Leo. He's an old guy who wears nineteen-seventies, polyester jumpsuits. He won't be too hard to find." Sinclair kissed him, told him she'd see him later then headed for the car.

When Sinclair got into the car, she repeated to Ardelia what Bruce had told her. Since there were only a couple of hours left in the work day, Ardelia took Sinclair to talk to Marge. As Sinclair was getting out of the car, she turned to Ardelia, asking, "What the hell am I supposed to say to this lady?"

"I don't know, shit, wing it."

Sinclair proceeded to the elevator, shaking like she was naked in sub zero weather. When she stepped off the elevator she could see Marge at her desk. She proceeded toward Marge with caution. By the time she reached Marge's desk, two maintenance men had walked up. Before Sinclair could speak, Marge held up one finger, indicating that she should wait to speak.

"Marge, we're here to change the locks and pack up Ms. Evan's office," one of the large, burly men said.

"Go ahead. The door is unlocked."

Marge turned her attention back to Sinclair, but while Marge was turned away, Sinclair saw the stop pay notice on Marge's desk. After seeing the notice and hearing that the office was being packed and the locks changed, Sinclair was more jittery than before. Marge asked her for the third time; "May I help you?"

"Uh, well, uh, I was here to see Cynthia Evans, but it looks like she no longer works here."

"What is the nature of your business? Could one of the other partners help you?"

Sinclair was too stunned to respond, but she sure as hell didn't want to speak to one of the partners. She managed to get her feet to finally move. She scurried off to the elevator without looking back. When she got outside, she didn't see Ardelia. Just as panic was starting to set in, Ardelia honked and waved from across the street. Sinclair raced across the street and hopped into the passenger's seat. She leaned forward, resting her head on the dashboard. She raised her head as she started to tell Ardelia what she'd learned.

"You are not going to believe this!" Sinclair said, her voice quivering.

"Tell me! You're scaring me."

"They've fired Cynthia."

"What? No, that can't be. What makes you say that?"

"I saw a stop pay notice to payroll on Marge's desk. The maintenance crew came while I was standing there. They were about to pack Cynthia's office and change the locks!"

"Oh my God! How do I tell Cynthia this? She's going to snap."

Ardelia started the car and slowly pulled out into traffic. Several miles from the office, Ardelia spotted the black Yukon in her rearview mirror. By the time she told Sinclair to look, the Yukon had disappeared, but the silver Navigator was now on their tail. They played cat and mouse for a bit, then Ardelia made a few, short, quick turns, and got rid of them. The news Sinclair had given her made her head straight for home. They'd forgotten about going to Syncopations until the turns Ardelia made ended them up on the street that Syncopations was on. They parked in front and went in.

They took a seat at a table in the corner, while they got a feel of the place. Sinclair looked around for a polyester jumpsuit, but she saw five or six of them.

"Damn, don't they know what year it is?"

"Not only are the jumpsuits outdated, but they're too small. Lord, what are we in store for?" Ardelia sarcastically stated.

Sinclair didn't want to approach the group of polyester kings, so she went to the bar and asked the bartender which one was Leo. She asked him if he could get Leo to come to their table. A couple of moments later Leo was at their table. Before sitting, he introduced himself and ordered a round of drinks.

Naturally, he was curious as to why two young, attractive women were asking for him, so he started the conversation.

"What's your reason for seeking me out?"

"We seem to be tangled up in a situation that has gone way beyond our comprehension. My husband, Bruce, told me to come see you."

"Bruce? I don't know anyone named Bruce."

"I'm sorry, I forgot that only family calls him by his real name. You probably know him as Blade."

"Yeah, yeah. I know Blade. He's an investigator. He does a lot of work for Savonte'. So why did he send you to me?" Ardelia chimed in to sum it all up.

"Savonte' convinced my girlfriend to become a partner in his real estate business. Since she became a partner she has been in a terrible car accident and is laid up for a while. She gave Savonte' control of her finances and he has wiped out her bank accounts, turned off the utilities at her house and we believe that he is trying to sell her house. We also believe he has convinced the partners at her architectural firm that she's embezzled money from the firm. She's lost her job and doesn't have a dime in the bank, all at the hands of Savonte'."

"Basically, she's completely destroyed and we don't know why he's done this to her," Sinclair added.

"Uh huh, sounds all too familiar," Leo remarked.

"How so? Ardelia asked.

"I used to be a partner in that group many years ago. Only, at that time, there were some different players. The fella who started the group is now a silent partner and Savonte' is the lead man. He's only the lead man as a front though. The silent partner calls the shots and Savonte', Evan and Tony execute his orders. That son of a bitch behind the scenes caused me to lose a great deal of money, but I was able to get out before he destroyed me."

"So this other person is the one who wants my friend destroyed? Sinclair asked.

"I haven't been in the mix with them for a very long time, but I would imagine so," Leo replied.

"Do you know Catherine Garrett? She seems to somehow be connected to all of this."

"Aw, yeah, Cat and I go way back. She's his aunt."

"His aunt? Who, Savonte'?"

"No, the silent partner."

"Who is this silent partner?" Ardelia asked again.

"You need to tread lightly before going forward. Don't try to deal with him without careful planning."

"I don't mean to pry, but can you please tell me who we're dealing with? The suspense is making me crazy," Ardelia begged.

"His name is..."

Before Leo could spit the name out, Savonte' came strolling through the front door. Leo eased his business card across the table to Ardelia. He kept his eye on Savonte' hoping he didn't see him talking to Ardelia and Sinclair.

"Call me," he spoke softly, as he got up to leave. He eased his way around the room and back to his usual spot without Savonte' noticing.

Ardelia and Sinclair tried to ease out too, but Savonte' spotted them leaving. He followed them out, questioning why they were there. Once again Sinclair was nervous, but Ardelia showed no fear.

"We've been over twenty-one for a long time. We don't need your permission to have a drink," Ardelia snarled.

"I've never seen you in here before, Sinclair. Shouldn't you be home playing nurse?"

"There's a first time for everything."

"Uh huh," Savonte' grunted as he turned to go back inside.

Ardelia always managed to make his blood boil and he was

much too cool to stand on the sidewalk having a schoolhouse, verbal brawl. Ardelia wanted to conk him in the back of his head with her shoe, but Sinclair took her by the arm and led her to the car.

Ardelia gunned the motor before putting the car into gear. She pulled out so fast, the rear of the car fish tailed. She was angry as hell and Sinclair's timid docile behavior was getting on her nerves. Plus, she dreaded having to tell Cynthia more bad news.

When they pulled into the driveway, Ardelia couldn't bring herself to get out of the car. Her chest tightened, her palms became clammy and sweat trickled down her face. Sinclair looked at Ardelia with puppy dog eyes, which infuriated Ardelia. She didn't have the time or the energy to hold her hand. She needed all of her strength to keep her best friend from becoming suicidal. Ardelia rolled her eyes at Sinclair, got out of the car and slammed the door. Sinclair scampered closely behind her.

When they walked into the house, Cynthia was sitting on the sofa in the family room. She smiled as they entered the room, expecting to hear that they had found out enough to solve the bazaar happenings. However, Cynthia sensed trouble when she looked at Ardelia. The vibe she felt was creepy. She knew then that the news wasn't good, but she never imagined how bad things were. Sinclair sat on the love seat and Ardelia sat next to Cynthia.

"I can tell something's wrong, very wrong, Ardelia. Tell me what's going on."

Ardelia took a deep breath and tried to talk, but nothing

would come out. Cynthia looked to Sinclair and said, "Somebody better tell me something, you guys are scaring me. Since Ardelia won't talk, then you tell me, Sinclair."

Ardelia looked at Sinclair and shook her head. Sinclair knew it had to be told delicately and she didn't know Cynthia well enough, plus she was too mousy to tell it right. Ardelia sucked it up and began to tell Cynthia how the events unfolded throughout the day.

Cynthia's face turned flush as Ardelia told her everything they'd learned. She didn't scream or cry. Actually, she was handling it so well Ardelia was concerned that she was teetering on the edge. There was no way that Cynthia should have been so calm. It wasn't as if she was embarrassed to cry in front of Sinclair, since Sinclair had seen her cry before.

When Ardelia finished her version of the events of the day, Cynthia asked Ardelia to make sure she picked Chris up from her friend's house while she was at therapy. She also asked Ardelia if she would take Chris school shopping, since school would be starting in a couple of weeks.

"Why don't we wait for you to come back from therapy and we go together?"

"No! Would you please just take care of her for me?" Cynthia barked as she headed to her bedroom.

Ardelia told Sinclair that Cynthia was acting strangely and that she was really worried about her. "I have to keep my eye on her," Ardelia said solemnly.

"What do you need me to do?"

"Nothing . . . there's really nothing you can do. I'm going to try to contact Leo sometime tomorrow. Come on, let me take you to your hotel."

CHAPTER SEVENTEEN

17

As the days slowly passed, Cynthia recovered rapidly.

She pushed herself hard in physical therapy and she could now walk without her cane. Chris returned home and got geared up for the first day of school. Ardelia had repeatedly called Leo, but hadn't been able to reach him, nor had they heard from Sinclair in several days. The last time they were all together, Ardelia made Sinclair feel unwanted, so Sinclair refused to call.

Cynthia hadn't mentioned anything about the disastrous events in her life. She had totally shut down and closed herself off from everyone. She talked to Chris, but only when Chris struck up a conversation. Ardelia gave Cynthia the space she felt Cynthia needed, but she monitored her closely. They muddled around the house like robots. There was no joy or laughter at all.

As the first day of school rolled around, Chris was anxious to see her buddies she hadn't seen for a while. She was dressed forty-five minutes earlier than she needed to be. She went downstairs to talk to her mom before leaving for the day.

"Why don't you have on one of your new outfits?" Cynthia asked.

"That is not cool, Mom," Chris replied and started laughing.

Cynthia needed to see her child smile. She grabbed her and hugged her tightly. As she released her embrace, she held Chris' face with both hands and asked, "You know how much I love you, don't you?"

Chris nodded her head.

"You know that even though I've made some very poor choices, I would never do anything to intentionally hurt you, don't you?"

Chris once again nodded her head.

"I promise you that I'm going to get our lives back. It may be a little tough at first, but I need for you to be strong. No matter what, try to stay focused on school and continue to get good grades. Will you do that for me?"

As Chris nodded for the third time she asked, "What's wrong Mom, you're scaring me?"

As the tears filled Cynthia's eyes and dropped onto her cheeks, she shook her head and responded, "Nothing...nothing's wrong. I'm going to make everything right. I want you to keep that in mind everyday until the sun shines on our lives again, okay?"

They hugged tightly until Ardelia came in to tell Chris that it was time to go. Cynthia kissed Chris on her forehead and then blew her a kiss as she walked to the door.

The school wasn't very far away, so Ardelia returned home rather quickly. When she came into the house, Cynthia called her into the family room.

"Ardelia, do your parents still have that old Mercedes that they never used to drive?"

"Yeah, why?"

"I was wondering if they'd let me use it for a while."

"Probably, but I don't know what kind of condition it's in."

"As long as it starts and goes forward and backward, I can't be too concerned about much else. I need to be able to get around without being chauffeured."

"Has the doctor said that you can drive?"

"Yes," she replied in an irritated tone.

"Excuse me for being concerned. I'll call them now."

Ardelia made the call to her parents and they were willing to lend the car to Cynthia. Cynthia told Ardelia to let them know she'd have the therapist drop her there after her therapy session.

"I could take you by there, Cynthia."

"Thanks, but I've leaned on you far too much and far too long. I have to get my life back. If you'll see to Chris, I'd be most appreciative."

Ardelia looked at Cynthia strangely, realizing that something didn't feel right. She couldn't put her finger on it, but Cynthia was up to something.

Ardelia decided not to push the issue and went upstairs to her bedroom. A short time later the med van was out front and Cynthia rolled a large luggage bag to the door. The therapist met her at the door and carried the luggage to the van, while Cynthia made her way down the steps.

By the time Ardelia came back downstairs, the van was pulling out of the driveway. As she watched the van drive away, she feared what Cynthia was planning to do. Ardelia sat around for hours worrying about the horrors that seemed to wait around every corner.

Finally, as morning turned into afternoon, Ardelia decided to try reaching Leo again. Luckily, he answered on the second ring.

"Leo!" Ardelia said with excitement.

"This is Ardelia. I met you the other day at Syncopations. I've been trying to reach you for days."

"Hey there, what's up?" Leo replied in a dry tone.

"I'm still trying to find out the name of this silent partner you mentioned. Will you still help me?"

"I've thought about this a great deal since we spoke and I really don't want to get involved."

"Please don't do this. My friend's life is unraveling and the only way we can stop it, is to know the source. Please just give me the name and I promise not to bother you again," she begged.

Leo briefly hesitated then responded.

"Okay, but once I give you the name you're on your own. I will not give you any more information and I will not get involved. Is that one hundred percent clear?"

"Yes, yes, just give me the name."

Ardelia couldn't believe her ears. She was mortified. Her mouth fell open and her body quaked with anger and fear. Just as she repeated the name..."Thomas! Thomas Alexander!" Leo hung up the phone.

Damn! Thomas left town, but he's been destroying Cynthia little by little. I have to let Cynthia know.

Ardelia phoned her parents house and when her father answered, she said, "Daddy, when Cynthia comes to pick up the car, ask her to call me immediately."

"You just missed her. She left about ten minutes ago. She's probably on her way there."

Ardelia paced the floor, checking the window every few seconds. Waiting for Cynthia to pull up in the driveway seemed like an eternity. As the time ticked away, her head pounded with pain and she realized it was time to get Chris from school. As she jumped in the car, she thought to call Cynthia on her cell phone.

"The number you have reached is not in service. Please check the number and try again," the recording announced.

Damn it. Her cell phone has been disconnected, too," Ardelia thought as she tossed the phone onto the passenger seat. She waited for Chris in front of the school, but was in a daze. Chris knew something was wrong when she got in the car. Ardelia was hoping that Cynthia was at the house by the time they got back. However, when they drove into the cul-de-sac her parents' Mercedes was nowhere in sight.

They went on into the house and Ardelia tried her best to act normal. Chris went into Cynthia's room to tell her about her day.

"Where's my mom?" she asked Ardelia.

"The doctor gave her the go ahead to drive, so she went to pick up my parents' extra car."

"Cool. When will she be back?"

"I don't know. I haven't talked to her since she left this morning."

"Okay, I'll call her on her cell." Chris said nonchalantly. Ardelia let her dial the number so that she didn't have to tell her the phone was disconnected. Chris got the same recording that Ardelia had gotten.

"Why's my mom's phone disconnected?"

"I'm not sure, honey," Ardelia replied without looking at her.

"Oh boy, here we go again."

"What do you mean by that, Chris?"

"She's acting weird like she did when we lived with Thomas. Stuff is happening and nobody's telling me anything."

"I don't know what to tell you, other than whatever your mom does she'll never stop loving you."

"Yeah, whatever."

"I'm here for you, no matter what."

"She's got wheels now?"

"Yeah, so?"

"She won't be back anytime soon."

"Why would you say that?"

"Forget it. I won't look for her," Chris remarked as she turned to leave the kitchen.

"Where are you going?"

"To my room."

"You're not going to eat?"

"Nope, I'm not hungry. I'll see you in the morning," she said in a pitiful tone.

Ardelia flopped down into the kitchen chair and laid her head on the table. She was mentally exhausted and drifted off to sleep.

By the time Ardelia awakened, night had fallen. She went upstairs to see what Chris was doing and found her curled up in the fetal position in the center of the bed. Ardelia draped a blanket over her and watched her sleep for a bit, but as tears overcame her she left the room. She went downstairs and logged onto the computer to get a background search on Thomas, but came up empty. She then conducted a search on Catherine Garrett.

"Now we're cooking. Let me print this out and give it a good read," she mumbled to herself.

Halfway through the report, something startling jumped out at her. She held her chest with one hand and covered her mouth with the other.

I have to be dreaming. This shit is too crazy *to be real. This is some 'I Spy', '007' kind of shit. Catherine Garrett's business is a* *subsidiary to the real estate business, and, looking at the family tree,* *she's related to Thomas. What the hell??!* Ardelia thought.   She decided to go see Cynthia's Aunt Lucille the next day. She needed to know if she'd heard from Uncle Bobby and where he might be. Finding Uncle Bobby would put her closer to Thomas. Plus, she didn't think going to Catherine would do much good. She planned to see Catherine as a last resort.

Ardelia finally called it a night when Cynthia hadn't come home by eleven-thirty. She climbed into bed, but she couldn't go to sleep. She waited for morning, but the seconds, minutes and hours seemed to move slower than ever. Ardelia was lying on her back waiting for the sun to acknowledge the day. When the sun finally did come up, she popped up and headed down the hall to Chris' room. Chris was already awake and in the shower. Ardelia went back to her bedroom to shower and dress as well.

They met up in the kitchen about forty-five minutes later.

"So, did my mom come home?"

Ardelia dropped her head and reluctantly replied, "No."

"Humph, just what I thought. I'm ready to go. I'll meet you by the car.

Chris flung her backpack over her shoulder, stuck a donut in her mouth and walked out of the kitchen. When Ardelia got to the car, Chris was leaning on the passenger door chomping on the donut. Chris had an attitude, but Ardelia decided not to scold her since she was only acting out her feelings for her mother.

　　She dropped Chris off at school and went to see Aunt Lucille. When she knocked on the dilapidated, wooden door, a woman she'd never seen before answered the door. The woman was four feet eight or so, about one hundred eighty pounds, dressed in a white nurse's uniform. Apparently she was a live-in, caring for Cynthia's Aunt Lucille.

　　Ardelia stepped into the house, observing the poor conditions Aunt Lucille was living in. Since Aunt Lucille was bedridden, the hospital bed was set up downstairs in the back room. Aunt Lucille was having trouble speaking when Cynthia last saw her, but her condition had gotten worse. The nurse was accustomed to translating and speaking for Aunt Lucille, so Ardelia directed her questions to the nurse. Aunt Lucille grunted and blinked uncontrollably. The nurse patted Aunt Lucille's hand in an effort to calm her, then replied as she held her hand.

　　"She's responding like this because we buried him last week."

　　"Buried him?"

　　"Yeah, she got a call a few weeks ago that her husband had been found dead in some little place in Iowa. His body was sent back here and we had a very small service at the funeral home."

　　"Found dead? In Iowa? What the hell was he doing in Iowa?"

　　"I'm not sure. I was sent here by the agency when he left her alone. A neighbor called family services and I've been here ever since."

"So was he sick and died alone, or was there foul play?"

"Well, the police called, but since she couldn't talk, and I wasn't a family member, they wouldn't tell me anything. So I can't answer that question, either."

Ardelia leaned over the bed and kissed Aunt Lucille on her cheek. She thanked the nurse and headed toward the front door. As she turned the doorknob, the nurse blurted out, "Hey, wait a minute. There was a guy named Frank who came by here a few weeks ago and I gave him Bobby's address and telephone number that I had found laying on the kitchen counter. If you know Frank, he might be able to help you."

"Frank's dead, too," Ardelia said sorrowfully, as she walked out and closed the door behind her. She sat in the car thinking, before she pulled off. *That's why they killed Frank. He was getting too close to Thomas.*

Ardelia went home feeling defeated once again.

In downtown Chicago, Cynthia was going door to door applying for jobs. She'd been job hunting since eight-thirty a.m., but hasn't gotten one bite. Billie had made sure that everyone in the business knew that she'd been fired and why. Surely, at the executive level, Cynthia had been blackballed in every industry. The only job she'd get would involve hot grease and a drive-through window. It hadn't dawned on her that the partners had blackballed her so she kept applying. She had promised Chris that everything was going to be all right. She was determined to keep that promise. She wanted to be the light in her child's life and she knew she had to make some money to make it happen.

Days went by and still no luck. She was getting by on a few hundred dollars she had in her purse and two credit cards that weren't maxed out. Those measly pickings would only float her for a few more days. Each day that came, Cynthia tried harder and harder to become employed.

One place where she'd applied was impressed with her resume and set up an interview with her for the next day. At that point, she stopped looking so she'd be at her best for the interview.

She wanted to call and check in with Chris, but she decided to wait until she could tell her child that she'd landed a job. She also didn't want to answer any questions until she had something to tell. If she'd known Ardelia had so much helpful information, she would have called. She went to bed early, anxiously awaiting the interview. Cynthia arrived for the interview thirty-minutes early, but was told that the person who set up the interview was out sick. Come to find out the lady who set up the interview was an office associate. She wasn't a decision maker nor did she have the authority to conduct an executive interview without input from one of the executives. The receptionist buzzed one of the partners and explained the dilemma.

The partner was familiar with Cynthia, but had already been tipped off by an executive at another firm about her situation, so he had to have the tough conversation with Cynthia. He informed Cynthia that the associate had scheduled the interview in error. He told her that they had already filled the position and apologized for her inconvenience. She thanked him for his time and returned to her hotel.

Cynthia sat on the bed and counted her remaining money and realized that she needed to move to a motel in order to stretch her dollars. Her credit cards had enough available to at least get checked in. She checked out of the nice, clean hotel, then drove until she saw a sign that read; *$24.99 a day, with cable.* She pulled into the parking lot, but looked around before getting out of the car. The neighborhood was a little seedy, but she could no longer afford to stay in the higher priced hotels she was accustomed to. As she turned to open the car door, a filthy, mangy panhandler was standing at the car door with his hand out. Although polished, educated and formerly successful, she was not afraid of these surroundings. She could function in any environment she had to. At this point she was merely trying to survive. The rinky-dink, little hole-in-the-wall motel was only a stepping stone. She pushed the car door open and sent the panhandler on his way. She was as needy as he was, and she wasn't willing to give him some of her last few crumbs.

She went inside, checked in and paid for one week on her credit card. This way she knew she had shelter for at least a week. She went to the corner store to buy cleaning supplies, soda and chips. When she returned from the store, she rolled her luggage into the room, then immediately sprayed the sheets, the toilette, and the carpet with disinfectant. She thoroughly cleaned the bathroom, then flopped onto the bed and gazed out the window. She turned on the television and dozed off.

About an hour later, there was a knock at the door. She was so out of it, she didn't hear the knock at first. Once again, there was incessant knocking at the door. Cynthia started to come around, opening one eye, hoping the knock was part of a dream. This time the knocks came harder and more rapidly. She rolled out of the bed and onto her feet. She couldn't imagine who it could be since no one knew that she was there. She snatched the door open and let her attitude greet the visitor.

"Hey, who are you?" the knocker asked.

"Who are you looking for?" Cynthia replied.

"Uh, I was lookin' fo' Sugarfoot," the knocker said with slurred speech.

"Who or what the hell is a Sugarfoot?"

"She been stayin' here fo' a while" he said, once again with a slur.

"Well, she's not here any longer."

As the tattered, frail man opened his mouth to speak again, Cynthia slammed the door in his face. He stepped to the right and pressed his face against the window. Cynthia reached up to close the blinds and the raggedy ass blinds fell to the floor. She called the front desk and asked the clerk to come up and fix or replace it.

"Lady, you ain't at the Hilton. It is what it is. Deal with it."

The dial tone sounded before Cynthia could open her mouth to respond.

"Rude motherfucker."

She snatched the bedspread off of the bed and attempted to rig the bedspread to cover the window. As shabby as it may have looked, it covered the window, for the moment anyway. Cynthia could still see the shadow of the seedy looking man through the bedspread, but eventually he moved on. She stretched herself across the bed and gazed into space. As she lay there thinking about finding a job, it dawned on her that the partners must have put her on a blackball list. Her credentials were too impressive to be turned down everywhere she applied. She didn't want to be reduced to a functionary when she was accustomed to calling the shots. At any rate, she planned to keep looking for something that was more of a fit, rather than settle for some mindless position. While she lay there, night began to fall. Other than the weird man who had come to the door, it had been pretty quiet and peaceful. The later it got, the peace and quiet turned into a jungle and she began to hear loud conversations, music and honking horns.

She got out of bed and peeked out the window from behind the rigged window covering. She could hardly believe what she saw. The parking lot that was nearly empty when she arrived was filled with cars. Earlier, the only people she'd seen were the desk clerk, the panhandler and the man who came to her door. Now, there were people everywhere. Actually, there were lots of women standing around and men sitting in and on cars. The women were skanky and sleezy looking, and wore long wigs, short tight dresses, and high heels.

The noise kept Cynthia from sleeping, so she threw on some clothes and went outside. She'd planned to get in her car and ride around for a while, but once she got outside, she was in the thick of it. After she was whistled at and groped by arms reaching out of car windows, she knew she had picked the wrong place to stay. She was in the midst of prostitutes and drug addicts. Even though she wasn't dressed in her usual Channel, her jogging suit was tasteful and she carried herself much differently than the other women around her.

The prostitutes gazed at her, knowing that she didn't belong. She was diverting the men's attention from the prostitutes without realizing it. Several of the prostitutes approached her and advised her to get lost. Instead of driving away in her car, she quickly returned to her room. She really didn't have any place to go and she surely didn't want to return in the wee hours of the morning to face them. The encounter really unnerved her, and she realized that she would have difficulty living this way. She still had high hopes that she would land a job that would allow her to return to the life she once knew.

She went to bed so she'd be rested for another day of job hunting, but she only tossed and turned the night away.

CHAPTER EIGHTEEN

18

As the start of another day began, Savonte' was

planning to deal with Mr. Anthony D'Amato. Savonte' couldn't forget how Tony had the nerve to tell him that he'd screwed him out of his money, and Savonte' thought of nothing but getting revenge. He grabbed his keys and headed to Tony's house on a serious mission.

When Savonte' got to Tony's house, he noticed a familiar car parked in front. He decided not to stop at that particular time. He figured he'd drive around for a bit and then double back later. Instead, he went to Syncopations for a drink.

While Savonte' sat at the bar sipping his drink, Leo came through the door. Leo sat at the bar next to Savonte' and shot the breeze with him. The bartender kept the drinks coming upon Savonte's request. Pretty soon, they both were pissy drunk. Savonte' had a stream of conscientiousness and started feeling guilty about all the dirt he'd done. He must have thought he was on a couch in a psychiatrist's office. Although his words were slurred and saliva was hanging from his bottom lip, he confessed to Leo how badly he felt about doing wrong to so many people. He went on and on until he thought about the woman he'd nicknamed Black Velvet Rose.

"Black Velvet Rose . . . I sure do miss her. We could have had something really great, but all I cared about was money. I didn't do right by her and I truly regret what I've done," Savonte' whined.

"Who is Black Velvet Rose? Sounds like a stripper's or a pole dancer's stage name," Leo commented.

"Nope. She was smart, funny and a real looker."

"You talk like she's dead, is she?"

"She may as well be, 'cause I fucked up. I fucked up her life so badly she'll never recover from it."

"Why'd you do it?"

"I was paid to."

"So..." Leo attempted to speak, but Savonte' shook his head and waved him off. Savonte' got up from the barstool, and staggered to the men's room. By the time he returned to the bar Leo had left. Savonte' sat at the bar with his head buried in his hands. He was frustrated and feeling sorry for himself. At this point he didn't want to seek revenge on Tony. The guilt of his past had come crashing down on him and he was starting to lose control. The bartender convinced him to stay until he sobered up.

About the same time, Cynthia was leaving the last place

where she had applied for a job. She'd been to five different places and damn near begged for a job. She was feeling as beaten down as anyone could feel. Her spirits were low and her confidence was a thing of the past. She had zero net worth, she had pretty much abandoned her child and she had no place to go, that is no place other than the drug and prostitute-infested motel. She drove as slowly as possible because she was in no hurry to get there any time soon.

By the time Cynthia pulled into the parking lot, she wished she had gotten there sooner. The parking lot was full and she had to park near an alley and walk quite a ways to reach her room. While she made her way through the throng of people, the prostitutes treated her as they had the day before. There was one who must have thought she'd been crowned queen of the prostitutes. She stepped in front of the steps to keep Cynthia from going up. Cynthia stopped and looked her up and down. Cynthia stepped to the side, turned sideways and went up the steps without making any contact with the queen. She went into her room, but when she clicked on the light, she found all of her things gone. There was nothing left except her personals in the bathroom and her underwear in the drawers. She raced to the bottom of the steps to confront the group that was standing there.

"Who took my shit? Which one of you brazen bitches took my fucking property?"

They all stared, but no one 'fessed up.

"I'll ask again. Who took my shit?"

"Don't nobody want shit you got, Ms. High Dollar Bitch."

"And who the hell are you?"

"I'm Joi and this is my girl Shell. Why?"

"If I see anybody wearing my shit I'm going to fuck them up."

Joi, Shell and the rest of the women started laughing. Cynthia was not amused, but didn't say anything else. She was fighting back the tears as she proceeded up the steps. A man was coming toward her as she got closer to the door to her room. He looked to be as much out of place as she did. He was clean cut and well groomed. He wasn't handsome, but he wasn't the ugliest thing she'd ever seen, either.

"Are you all right?" The man asked.

"Yeah, I'm fine."

When she turned the doorknob to go back into her room, he stepped to the door as well. She looked at him over her shoulder as if he had two heads. He held both hands up as though he was being arrested.

"Hey lady, I'm not going to harm you. We both seem to be down on our luck and out of place. I thought maybe we could be each other's ally."

"I'm sorry, but things in my life are so messed up I can't trust anyone."

"Well, would you like to go have a cup of coffee or a drink with me?"

Cynthia felt there was nothing to go back into the room for, so she agreed to have a drink with him. However, she wasn't comfortable enough to ride with him or him with her. She suggested she follow him wherever he wanted to go. They went a few blocks away to a nearby bar. They'd been there about thirty minutes before asking each other's name.

"So, what is your name?"

"I can't believe we've been sitting here this long without asking that question. It's Cynthia, yours?"

"Frederick, but everyone calls me Fred."

After a while, Fred had made Cynthia so comfortable, she tucked her problems away in the back of her mind. He made her laugh like she hadn't in quite some time and they stayed at the bar for hours. He told her damn near his whole life story, but she wouldn't go into any great detail about hers. She grazed over some things, but didn't tell it all. She was embarrassed by her situation, but also wanted someone in her new world to be comfortable with. She felt alone and disenchanted, but for some odd reason, Fred made her feel as though there was hope. Maybe this time she wasn't making a poor choice in friends. He wasn't rich or powerful or handsome, but he sure seemed to be a good guy. She definitely wasn't looking for a man, but being alone in that seedy motel made her desire a friend. She started to yawn, so Fred suggested they leave. She followed him back to the motel, and back to the parking space near the alley. He walked her to her room and she wasn't harassed this time. She invited him in and they watched television until Cynthia drifted off to sleep. Fred slipped her shoes off and covered her with the sheet. He watched a movie and then fell asleep, too.

Across town, sirens were blaring and police were crawling all around Tony's place. They'd roped off the perimeter of the house from the sidewalk to the front door. Savonte' had sobered up a little and was on his way back to Tony's. He was hoping that Janella had left so that he could deal with Tony man to man. Surprised couldn't describe what Savonte' felt as he approached the house and saw the police. There was no place to park in front of the house, so he parked at the corner and walked back to the house. Naturally, the police wouldn't let him past the yellow tape, but as he began to inquire about what had happened, he saw the coroner's people carrying a body in a body bag on a gurney.

"That can't be Tony! Is that Anthony D'Amato in that bag?" Savonte' asked the officer standing near the yellow tape.

"I don't know his name. It's the person who lives here. That's all I know."

Savonte' returned to his car and called Evan. He questioned Evan to see if he knew what was going on, but Evan had no answers. Savonte' rode around until almost dawn. Then he went home and drank himself into another stupor.

Their investment group was slowly falling apart. What used to be a lucrative business and close knit group was unraveling at the seams. They had become so complacent with their power and financial stability that they didn't prepare for times like these. They surely had never had disagreements over a woman, and never would have screwed each other out of money.

CHAPTER NINETEEN

19

A new day had begun and Cynthia was still asleep, so

exhausted she was snoring. Fred was sitting up in bed watching her sleep. Her snoring was driving him crazy, so he placed his hand over her mouth to stop the snoring. The contact to her face caused her to jump and start swinging. Fred calmed her down and let her know that she wasn't in any danger. She cuddled up next to him and drifted right back to sleep.

He rubbed her back while he flipped through the television channels. The slow, gentle caressing began to arouse her. She reached for his face and pulled him to her and then began to passionately kiss him. Although the passion existed, Fred wasn't able to respond to her in a natural way. He was hot and bothered, but unable to become erect. Cynthia soon realized that he was a limp noodle, but she was sensitive to his helplessness, so she stopped. He had been so kind to her that there was no way she was going to make him feel any worse than he already did, so she laid with her head on his chest.

It's a good thing he's been nice to me or I would have told him off and put him out of here. I feel terrible that I reached out to him, but I was half sleep and I wasn't thinking. If I hadn't kissed him, he wouldn't have tried to respond. Poor thing. He's a wet firecracker, a dud. Um, um, um... that's too bad," she thought as she came crashing down.

"Fred. I should probably get up and shower so I can get my day started. What are you going to do today?"

"I don't have any plans. I thought we could hang out."

"I really appreciate that, but I have to stand on my own."

"Helping you out ain't stopping you from standing on your own."

"You know, I'm at a point that I may have to stand in the parking lot at night with those bitches to be able to eat."

"Be a prostitute!? You have too much class for that."

"Hell, I may as well get paid for it, instead of lying down for free."

"That's not what I'm saying. I mean if you have to resort to that, be a call girl, not a street walking, ten dollar prostitute."

"Same thing."

"No it isn't. A prostitute walks the streets, but call girls drive expensive cars. That ain't the same thing."

"Okay, but a call girl sure as hell ain't being called on at this tacky ass motel."

"True, but I know a place downtown where all the high rollers go. Politicians, doctors and lawyers go there for some fun."

"Well, unfortunately my credit cards are tapped out and I'm too low on cash to get an expensive room for one night in a high dollar hotel these days."

"I'll pay for one week on my credit card and buy you a couple of nice outfits, but that's all I can do. You can pay me back one day when you get on your feet."

Cynthia looked at him in amazement. She couldn't believe this stranger was willing to help her, but at what cost? Everything he said seemed genuine, but she'd heard genuine before and it turned out to be trouble.

She thought for a moment about the reality of her situation. If he disappeared tomorrow she'd be without a place to stay, no money, no credit and prostituting in the parking lot for ten or twenty dollars. This seemed to be the better option, so she took him up on his offer.

They showered, she gathered her personals and they left for downtown. She followed him so that she didn't have to leave the car behind. Fred pulled into the covered parking lot under the hotel and Cynthia followed closely behind. They parked and headed up on the elevator.

First, they stopped at the registration desk to get her checked in. While Fred paid, Cynthia looked around to check out her new surroundings. She was very pleased with her new place to stay, but she knew it would only be for a week, if she didn't make some money quickly.

Fred handed her the room key, then took her by the hand. He led her across the lobby into an attached mini mall. Her eyes lit up and twinkled like stars on the darkest night. She loafed around, pretending like it didn't matter if she got anything or not, when actually she was so glad to be shopping she didn't know what to do. She was more grateful to Mr. Limp Noodle than she let on.

She was used to buying whatever she pleased, without caring about the price tag, but she wanted to be mindful of his kindness, plus she knew how to bargain shop. She looked for the best thing she could find on sale. By her standards he had given her a pretty low budget to work with, but Fred suggested she choose sexier selections. Out of habit, she was buying as if she was going to the office.

"Silly me, I forgot I wasn't in an office anymore. Maybe I should just buy lingerie and call it a day," Cynthia snapped sarcastically.

"Whoa, hang on there. If I were in a bar or in a hotel looking for a lady friend for the evening, I would choose the one showing a little leg, not the one in a business suit."

"A call girl doesn't have to show and tell until it's time to show some tail, but I get your point. I'll look for sexy. I'll need a pair of shoes and some pretty underwear. Are you going to get those too?"

"Sure, I can do that."

What's your real angle? Why are you doing this for me? I'm not going to turn you down, but I'm going to keep my eye on you, she thought.

She put the suits back and started to look for something sexy. She had plenty of sexy things in her closet at home, so she knew what to look for. She looked for her favorites, chiffon and silk as she held up a vibrant, red silk dress.

"Yeah, that's what I'm talking about. You'll attract a lot of attention in that."

She held up another one and he liked it too. She could tell that he was getting a kick out of watching her shop. It was as if he envisioned her in the dress, but he couldn't do anything if he got her alone, so what was the point? She milked it anyway, leaving with six new dresses. *Shit, he said the budget was low, but he spent a pretty penny.*

After finding a pair of sandals with straps and underwear, they went up to her room. Cynthia bounced on the bed, delighted to have a clean bed to sleep in, not to mention there wouldn't be loud music and hookers hanging out outside of her door. She looked at her clothes and smiled. It was amazing to see how a little could make her smile, after the beating she'd taken in the last few weeks. She gave Fred a puzzling look.

"What? What's wrong?"

"How the hell am I supposed to be a call girl without any contacts? If I sit in the hotel bar picking up men, it'll be the same as picking up men on the corner. We make the perfect pair. Dumb and Dumbette."

"Hold on a minute. I know a few guys with money who see call girls on a regular basis. One of them doesn't even want sex. He just likes to spend time with pretty women. He wants to lay in the bed, look, touch and talk."

"He sounds like a pervert."

"If my friend can hook you up with him and one other one, you'll be set."

Hmmmm, how convenient. You have all the answers for a little man who can't get a hard on. I don't have much choice, so I guess I'll deal with these people long enough to get myself financially back on track. Maybe the other one will be impotent, and I won't have to do anything but spend time with them, Cynthia thought.

"Hand me the phone," Fred requested.

One phone call was all he needed to make.

"Hey Sterling, what's up with you these days?"

"Fred? Man, I haven't talked to you in a long time. What gives?"

"I have a lady friend looking to get together with a nice man or two."

"Are you talking about what I think you're talking about?"

"Yeah, you game?"

"That's not my thing anymore, but I can get her a couple of new friends. She's not a bow wow, is she?"

"Not a chance. Classy and striking…they won't be disappointed."

"Alright. Let me make a couple of calls. Where can I call you?"

"312 555 4800. Room 410."

"I'll call you back shortly."

Fred explained to Cynthia that Sterling was calling a couple of contacts, too.

"You look a little uncomfortable, Cynthia. Are you all right with this?"

"As all right as I can be. I guess I have to be all right. I need money and this seems to be my only option. It won't be a whole lot different than screwing somebody for free."

"You're sure? 'Cause I can call him back and tell him to forget about it."

"No. I'll get drunk to numb myself. I just hope they're not critters."

She blew out a lung full of air, lying back on the fluffy pillows. Fred sat twiddling his thumbs, waiting for Sterling to call back.

A short time later the phone rang. Fred answered on the second ring. Sterling had contacted both of his friends, and they were both interested in meeting Cynthia. She told Fred to tell Sterling to give the hotel number to them and she would handle it from there.

She didn't want to be bothered tonight though. She wanted to relax in the bathtub and enjoy a good night's sleep, in a clean, safe place. Fred left shortly after they finished talking to Sterling and Cynthia went straight to the bathtub.

She stretched out, relaxing in the tub for almost an hour, then returned to the bed. She ordered room service and had it charged to the room. Twenty-six dollars wasn't going to kill Fred's credit card, so she figured she'd pay it back with the rest of the money she owed him.

After she ate, she snuggled under the covers to watch a movie. As she began to drift off to sleep the telephone rang.

"Hello," she answered.

"Is this Cynthia?"

"Yes," she replied as she sat up in the bed.

"I got a call from Sterling. Can you talk?"

"Yes. So when can I meet you?"

"Would tomorrow work for you?"

"Yes, that's fine. What time?"

"About seven?"

"I'll meet you in the bar downstairs. How will I know you?"

"Sit at the bar, on the end near the piano. I'll come to you."

"Okay, I'll see you tomorrow."

When Cynthia hung up the phone, she struggled with her predicament. She would either have to get comfortable with being a call girl or go without food and a place to stay. She weighed her options and, naturally, money and comfort outweighed starvation and homelessness. She smoked a cigarette and went to sleep.

CHAPTER TWENTY

20

"Yes, everything here has been taken care of.

What happened to that Tony fella? I was asked to make sure the paperwork fell into the right hands to get Cynthia fired for embezzlement, but no one was supposed to get hurt."

"Calm down. Nothing will come back to you. That wasn't planned, but it became necessary."

"I have another call coming in. I have to go."

"So do I, someone is at my door."

"Thank you for calling, Robinson, Cavil and Lee. How may I help you?"

"Marge. We need to meet when you get off work. Meet me at the restaurant across the street at five-thirty, okay?"

"Yes, I'll be there."

Marge went about her day, anticipating her evening meeting. The phones rang constantly and the partners kept her hopping.

Savonte' finally came out of his drunken stupor and he was very concerned about Tony's death. If Tony was operating scandalously with others, they might have killed him. Savonte' wanted to know what happened, so he planned to go to the police station to see what he could find out.

When Savonte' got to the police station, he was sent to see Detective Weaver. As he wandered down the hallway, he passed a room with a large inside window. After he passed the window of the room, he stopped and took a couple of steps back. He peered into the room and into the back of a woman's head. She was being interrogated by two detectives. He couldn't get a good enough view of the woman's profile, but she sure looked familiar. He shrugged it off and proceeded on to find Detective Weaver.

Once he got to the detective's desk, he was told that the detective was conducting an interrogation and he'd have to wait to see him. He was shown to a waiting area that happened to be directly across from the interrogation room that he'd passed earlier. He read a magazine while he patiently waited for the detective to finish.

Savonte' looked at his watch and realized he'd been waiting for nearly an hour. He put the magazine on the table and got up to leave. As he turned to go down the hallway, the door to the interrogation room opened. He stopped to see if he really knew the woman, or if his mind was playing tricks on him. Low and behold he did know her. It was Janella. She bowed her head as she was escorted out of the room. Savonte' stood in the hallway in shock as he watched her taken down the hallway. One of the detectives asked Savonte' if he could help him with anything. After collecting himself, he finally said, "Uh, yeah, I'm looking for Detective Weaver."

"That's me. What can I do for you?"

"I wanted to talk to you about my friend Anthony D'Amato. I went to his house and saw all the police. What happened to him?"

"He was murdered, but I can't discuss the details with you."

"Let me ask you this. Is Janella a suspect?"

"Oh, you know her?"

"Yes, is she a suspect?"

"Yes. She's our prime suspect and we are charging her with his murder. She's being booked right now."

"Awe, man. I can't believe this."

"Why don't you come and talk with me for a bit?" the detective suggested, as he placed his hand on Savonte's shoulder to guide him to his desk.

Detective Weaver asked Savonte' a multitude of questions. None of his answers helped the case, though. Savonte' was completely clueless as to what had happened. As Savonte' stood to leave he asked, "Is it possible for me to speak with Janella?"

"Not right now. She has made her one phone call and she needs to speak to legal counsel. A bail hearing has to be set. I guess if she's able to make bail, you could speak to her then."

Savonte' left the police station more baffled than when he arrived.

The workday was near an end and Marge prepared to leave for the day. Billie and Paulie stopped at Marge's desk as they were leaving for the day. They gave her a few more things to do and proceeded to the elevator.

I can't believe them. It's quitting time and they give me a day's work to do. I'll do this tomorrow." Marge thought with disdain.

She continued to tidy up and get ready to leave for the day. Within thirty minutes, Marge was walking out the door.

Marge and Catherine arrived at the restaurant at the same time. They walked through the door together and were seated immediately. As they ordered their first round of drinks, Billie and Paulie approached the table.

"Catherine, you and Marge know each other?" Paulie asked, curious.

"Yes," Catherine responded while Marge sat squirming in her seat. Marge was hoping neither of them would ask how they knew each other so she didn't have to explain anything, especially their relationship. But, unfortunately, that was the next question.

"How do you two know each other?" Billie queried.

Marge looked over to Catherine and Catherine to Marge.

"Don't speak at the same time," Paulie said sarcastically.

"She's my sister." Catherine replied boldly, not wanting to cower or look suspicious. They only knew Catherine because of the business she had with the firm, but Marge had to work for them everyday. Marge had to humble herself, but Catherine didn't.

"Really? Why didn't we know that?" Billie asked.

"There was no need to say. My dealings with the firm were always related to my business. It had nothing to do with my family tree," Catherine snapped.

"Oh, excuse me." Billie replied.

"We'll leave you to your family business then," Paulie said.

Billie and Paulie's table was across the room, so Marge and Catherine were able to speak freely. They talked about how well their plan had gone to get Cynthia fired, but then Marge mentioned Tony's death. She wanted to know how and why he had been killed. Catherine danced around Marge's question as long as she could, but Marge wouldn't let her off the hook. The explanation Catherine gave her was exactly what Janella had told her.

"Janella told me that Tony had figured out everything. He knew that Janella had used him for information and he also knew all the players involved. He'd stumbled upon more than he should have, and it put us all at risk. You know Janella well enough to know that she will do anything for her man. His identity was put in jeopardy; therefore she had to kill him. She called me this morning and told me what she'd done."

"I spoke to her this morning. I asked her about his death. She said nothing would come back on me and that someone was at her door," Marge revealed.

"That was the police. That's when they arrested her."

"Well, if nothing can come back on us, how did they go straight to her for the murder?"

"I don't have any details, but she either left something behind or someone saw her at his house. I really don't know."

"So where's her husband? Is he coming here to get her out of this mess?"

"Yeah, he'll be here later today or tomorrow."

They ate their meals then left for their homes. Billie and Paulie watched them leave and looked at each other with suspicion. Billie and Paulie didn't have a clue how manipulative Marge and Catherine had been. They had pulled off a frame up that was so well planned everyone believed it to be true.

Meanwhile, Blade was finally being released from the rehab center. Sinclair was on her way to pick him up and Ardelia had finally decided to check in on Sinclair, calling her on her cell phone.

"Hey, Sinclair. I wanted to check in with you to see how you're doing."

"Fine," Sinclair replied, with nothing else to say. She felt dismissed days ago and wasn't interested in playing in their game any longer. All Sinclair wanted was to get her husband and go home and put all the craziness behind them. She figured she'd leave Ardelia and Cynthia to their troubles and stay out of it.

Ardelia could feel the chilly vibe, but told Sinclair what she'd found out at Aunt Lucille's, anyway. She'd been holding it in about

Thomas since she hadn't been able to reach Cynthia. She had to get it off her chest and thought she could get Sinclair to talk to Blade about Thomas. Sinclair, on the other hand, wanted nothing to do with Ardelia or her issues. Sinclair felt tossed aside as if she was insignificant and that's where she preferred to stay.

"Blade is getting out of the rehab center today. I'm on my way to pick him up and I really don't want to burden him with any of this stuff right now. I was under the impression days ago that you didn't need me any longer, in fact, you didn't want me around any longer."

"That's not true. I've just had so much stuff going on I didn't know what to do." *Yes it is,* Ardelia thought.

"I understand, but I can't help you right now. I need to get my family back in order. I haven't been to my own house for sometime and I want to go home."

"All right," Ardelia replied.

The phone went dead.

Sinclair looked at her cell phone and then tossed it in the pocket under the stereo. *"Humph, think you can use me when you feel like it, then toss me aside on a whim? I don't think so,* Sinclair thought.

After finally arriving at the rehab center, Sinclair was excited to see Bruce. She parked and walked into the center with an upbeat stride. She passed a very handsome man as she proceeded to Bruce's room. They nodded a greeting to each other as he headed down the hallway and out of the center. Sinclair rounded the corner and into Bruce's room. He lay there in the bed, seemingly sound asleep.

"Hey, honey, ready to go?" Sinclair asked Bruce. There was no response. She walked over to the bed and shook him.

"Bruuuuce, wake uuuup," she said cheerfully, but she still got no response.

"Bruce! Bruce!" she yelled, as she grabbed his hand. When she let go of his hand, it fell onto the bed. He was dead!

"AAAAAAAAAAHHHHHHHHHHHHH!   Help!"   she screamed as she went running out of the room. "Somebody help me!" She saw a nurse, grabbed her by the hand and pulled her into Bruce's room. The nurse checked his pulse and remarked, "I'm sorry, ma'am, he's dead. He was fine an hour ago. I was in here to check his vitals before his release."

They looked at each other in amazement as Sinclair sat in the chair, hysterical with grief.

"How can this be? Call the police."

"I will after I call the doctor. We need to make sure there's a reason to call the police."

"A reason? A reason! He's fucking dead. What more reason do you need?"

"I know you're shocked, but there's a procedure we have to follow. The doctor should be the first one to check out a patient. His death could be medical related."

"You just checked him and hour ago, what medically could

have gone wrong that quickly?"

"Just let me do my job. We'll take care of this."

Sinclair sat there in a state of shock while the nurse called for the doctor. When the doctor arrived, they asked Sinclair to leave the room while the doctor checked him out. The doctor found no medical reason for his death, but he did find marks around his neck to indicate strangulation. He then called the police while Sinclair paced back and forth outside the room until the police got there.

The police questioned Sinclair to see what she could tell them that might help. She spent hours telling them about all the bazaar happenings, but everything sounded so far fetched, they didn't want to believe any of it had anything to do with Bruce's murder.

She left, feeling lonely and scared, so she sat in her car thinking. *Damn, I just cut Ardelia off at the knees and now I need her. I'm going to have to swallow my pride and call her. We both need each other, so maybe she'll talk to me."*

"Ardelia. I'm sorry for being nasty earlier. Can I come by and talk to you?" she asked pitifully.

"Yeah, I don't care." Ardelia said with an attitude.

Sinclair didn't want Ardelia to know right away what she needed her for. She wanted to see if Ardelia would allow her to come by before spilling her guts. She thought she'd wait until Ardelia told her what she needed before she told her about Bruce.

Sinclair pulled into Ardelia's driveway and checked her face for tear stains in the rearview mirror. She'd cried all the way there,

but didn't want Ardelia to know. She took a deep breath and
swallowed hard to collect herself. When Ardelia answered the door,
she was cold toward Sinclair. She stood in the doorway, pausing
before inviting her in. She thought for a moment about needing her
help, then softened a little. They went into the family room to talk.
Knowing that she didn't want to be the first to tell her story, Sinclair
asked Ardelia what she needed her for earlier. Ardelia went into
detail about Frank getting Uncle Bobby's address, then winding up
dead. She also told Sinclair that she'd spoken with Leo, and he had
revealed that the silent partner was Thomas.   Sinclair didn't
understand the connection with Thomas because she had no idea who
Thomas was or what he'd already done to Cynthia. Ardelia broke it
down for her and she started to get the picture. Ardelia went on and
on about this fine man then it clicked for Sinclair.

"Wait a minute! Hold on! The man you are describing was
at the rehab center today. I walked right past him!"

"He's dangerous as hell and I think he's behind all the shit
that's been happening."

"Oh, Shit!!!!. He must have killed Bruce!"

"Killed Bruce! What!?"

Sinclair broke down into tears.

"Yes, when I got to the rehab center Bruce was dead when I
got to his room. I had just passed this man and the nurse said
that Bruce was fine an hour before I got there."

Ardelia scratched her head and wondered how many more

had to die before this sick son of a bitch killed anybody else. She then thought about Chris. She needed to get her out of the house and some place safe from Thomas. He was crazy enough to get to Chris if all else failed. The walls were closing in on him if he had come back to town and that made him extremely dangerous. She hoped he would panic and make a mistake.

Meanwhile, Savonte' was at Syncopations slumped over at a table alone. He was drinking himself silly. He was distraught by Tony's death and Janella's arrest.

Hours later, Janella came strolling into Syncopations. She knew Savonte' would be there, so she looked for him as soon as she entered the club. She spotted him at the table and joined him. When he raised his head and noticed who'd sat next to him, he immediately started asking questions.

"What the hell is going on?"

"Nothing I can't handle."

"Why were you arrested for Tony's murder?"

"Cause I killed him."

"What? Are you kidding me? So you're prepared to go to jail?"

"Not a chance. He was meddling in something he shouldn't have been. My husband won't let me go to jail."

"What was he meddling in that could have cost him his life?"

"My business."

"What business? Your advertising firm?"

"No. Leave it alone."

"I can't."

"You should."

"What . . . or I'll be next?"

Janella shot Savonte' a glance that said *You bet.*

Savonte' got up from the table to leave.

"You're a sick bitch."

"I'll do anything for my man."

"Who's that?"

"You don't need to know. If you keep asking questions you'll find out. Leave it alone."

Savonte' shook his head and slowly left the club.

A short time later Ardelia and Sinclair showed up at Syncopations. They didn't know where else to go to find out more about Thomas. Ardelia had already told Sinclair that Leo wouldn't get involved. He made it very clear that once he divulged Thomas' name, he was not going to do anything else. They were hoping that Leo would give in, or that they would stumble up on someone else who could help. They realized it was a long shot, but they had no other options. Ardelia wanted to talk to Cynthia so badly, she was feeling sick. She didn't know if Cynthia was alive or dead. With so many others coming up dead, it was Ardelia's greatest fear that her friend might be dead, too.

Across the room Janella sat at a table with another man. They were huddled deep in the corner, in the dark, near the restrooms.

Ardelia and Sinclair sat at the bar in the open. They sure as hell didn't want to be secluded. While Sinclair and Ardelia drank sodas, Janella approached the bar. She ordered two drinks from the bartender.

"No one has come to our table to take a drink order in a while."

"I'll have the waitress bring your drinks to your table. What'cha drinkin'?"

"Tell her I'll have gin and seven and my husband will have a Maker's Mark."

Sinclair and Ardelia didn't have any idea who Janella was, so they didn't pay much attention to her. They hung out at the bar for about an hour longer and then decided to leave.

"I'd better go to the ladies room before we leave. This soda is going straight through me, Ardelia said."

"I'll go with you, said Sinclair."

After leaving the restroom, Ardelia looked at the couple in the corner and picked up her pace to leave. Sinclair scampered behind her trying to keep up. When they got to the sidewalk, Sinclair grabbed Ardelia by the arm.

"What are you doing? Why'd you go racing out of there?"

"That was Thomas in the corner with that woman!"

"What woman?"

"The one who came to the bar to order her drinks."

"She said she was ordering for herself and her husband.

Thomas is her husband?"

"Oh shit, must be. I HAVE to find Cynthia."

"How?"

"I don't know. I think I'm getting sick."

They sat in the car while Ardelia searched for aspirin in her purse.

Stumped, they drove back to Ardelia's to sit. They didn't know what else to do or where else to go.

CHAPTER TWENTY-ONE

21

At the hotel, Cynthia was getting ready for her date

with the mystery man. She had the red, silk dress laid out on the bed. She bathed and swept her hair up and clamped it with a nice hairpin. She was glad those bitches at the motel hadn't taken her toiletries. She had all of her personal stuff, which was necessary for getting dressed. She slipped into her lace underwear and her shoes. Once she put on her dress she was ready to leave. She added another squirt of cologne and walked out the door.

When she got to the lobby bar, she hesitated in the doorway before going in. She knew she had to do it, but butterflies fluttered in her stomach. After she took the first two steps, she was in stride. She held her head up and proceeded to the bar. She perched herself on the barstool and ordered a drink. When her drink arrived, she lit a cigarette and spun around to face the piano. The pianist was playing some mellow jazz that was very relaxing. She bobbed her head to the music while crossing her legs. She kept beat to the music by bouncing her top leg against her bottom leg. She'd been closed up in her room all day anticipating the night, so at this point she wasn't thinking about anything in particular. The music was so soothing she got lost in each note.

By now, she had finished her first drink and she turned around to order another. The bartender was running a tab, and she was hoping like hell that her date would not only show up, but pay it. While Cynthia waited for her next drink a raspy voice spoke to her over her shoulder.

"Hello. Are you Cynthia?"

She turned around to answer and was speechless. Actually, they were both speechless. Although she was surprised, she was glad that she'd always been nice to this man. It was one of the old polyester boys from Syncopations.

"Hey, there," she said, trying to cover up her embarrassment.

"Hey, I had no idea it would be you that I was meeting," Leo said surprised.

"Yeah, I guess not. We never knew each other's name," Cynthia responded as she dropped her head.

"There's no need for that," he said as he raised her chin with the tip of his finger.

"Okay," Cynthia said and smiled.

He ordered himself a drink and told the bartender to start a tab.

"I already did. You want me to add it to hers?"

"Yes, that'll be fine."

Whew… I don't have to worry about paying for the drinks and I'm damn sure going to need to be drunk to finish this night, Cynthia thought, relieved.

They chatted for a short time before he asked her to go to her room. He paid the bill, helped her down from the barstool and they went to her room. Cynthia was not on top of her game at all. Once again she hadn't asked the damn man his name.

"I know we've seen each other a lot, but what is your name?"

"Cleofus, but call me Leo."

Cleofus? Damn, who the hell named their child Cleofus? He has to be in his sixties with a name like that.

"Okay," she said, smiling.

Even though Cynthia was familiar with him, she wasn't comfortable knowing that she was going to have to go to bed with him. She didn't know if she was supposed to discuss price or what she was supposed to say. She decided to just ask.

"So Leo, since I've never done this before, what's the protocol?"

Leo laughed before responding.

"Well, I'm not a pimp or anything like that, but I only pay for your company. You don't have to have sex with me. Just get undressed and let me look at you. We can lay in the bed and talk. You probably need to talk, anyway."

I hope you're paying enough for me to stay in this hotel. Fifty or one hundred dollars ain't going to cut it, Cynthia thought before undressing.

"So, what do you pay for the time you spend?"

"Depends on the night, depends on the lady. I've paid as much as five thousand for one night. I've paid as little as one thousand for one night."

I want the five thousand. I guess I'll have to really pour on the charm to get five bills out of you, but okay.

At that moment, Cynthia slid the straps off of her shoulders, as Leo watched her dress fall to the floor. Her underwear was a one piece, red lace, body suit thong. As she turned to sit on the bed, her tattoo became the topic of conversation. Leo had her lay across the bed while he stroked the velvety tattoo with his finger.

"What made you get this?'

"Someone who was a part of my life at the time talked me into it."

"It's really pretty. It's so soft," he said dreamy eyed, as he stroked her butt cheek. He outlined it with his finger over and over again. Cynthia lay there wanting him to stop, but figured if she was going to get five thousand dollars at the end of the night, she could stomach him touching her tattoo. She laid her head on the pillow and relaxed. When she closed her eyes the room started to spin. She knew then that she was drunk enough to make it through the night.

"Black Velvet Rose," Leo mumbled.

Cynthia raised her head, and looked over her shoulder.

"What did you just say?"

"Black Velvet Rose," he repeated, with a look as if he'd said something wrong.

"Please don't call me that."

"Why not?"

"That asshole that talked me into getting this damn thing used to call me that. He was the only one who knew I had it and the only one who called me that. It brings back some very unpleasant memories."

"Oh shit. You're Black Velvet Rose?"

Cynthia sat straight up.

"What do you mean I'm Black Velvet Rose?"

"I was just talking to a fella at Syncopations who told me how he'd messed up Black Velvet Rose's life. He regretted what he'd done to her."

"What fella?"

"Savonte'."

"Motherfucker! That lousy son of a bitch has the nerve to have regrets. What else did he tell you?"

"He just said that he messed up your life."

"What did he do?"

"What didn't he do? He screwed me out of a lot of money in a real estate deal. He stole my money from my bank accounts. He refinanced my house and then sold it out from under me, with all the contents inside. And I was fired from my job as a partner in my architectural firm. I don't have a damn thing because of him. I'm in this room with you because I'm trying to get my life back."

"So you're the friend your girlfriend was talking about?"

"What girlfriend?"

"Umm," Leo said as he snapped his fingers trying to remember the name.

"Wait a minute. The name is coming to me. Ar..."

"Ardelia?"

"Yeah, that's it."

"When did you talk to Ardelia?"

"A few days ago when she was trying to find out about the silent partner in your real estate partnership and I told her."

"Who is it?"

"Shit. Here I go again. The silent partner is a guy that started the business when I was in it."

"You were in it? You used to be in partnership with Savonte', Evan and Tony?"

"There were other players at the time, but this particular person screwed me over just before I pulled out. I managed to get out before he bankrupted me. I bounced back before going under and now I have plenty of money, enough to go heads up with him."

"Who is it?" Cynthia asked nervously.

"Thomas..."

"Thomas Alexander!?"

"Yeah, you know him?"

Cynthia started to tremble and shake. Leo embraced her to keep her from coming unglued. When she ran down the history between the two of them, it infuriated Leo to know that Thomas had destroyed this woman's life over some childhood bullshit. He thought it was pretty low. After recalling how Thomas had done him, he told Cynthia he was willing to help her out. He told her that he would finance whatever she needed to get back on her feet and get revenge on Thomas.

They sat and talked for hours until Cynthia got a grip on herself.

Back at Ardelia's, she and Sinclair had decided to get out of the house. Ardelia wanted to just ride around and see what they'd luck up on. After riding in circles for a while, Sinclair suggested that they go to Marge's house. Sinclair knew that Ardelia would know where Marge lived, so Marge's house was there destination.

"So, when we get there what's the plan?" Ardelia asked.

"Hell, I don't know. She's the only one fragile enough to shake information from. We could strong arm her into telling us anything. What's your advice, wing it?"

"That's it. That's what we'll do."

They were two blocks away from Marge's house and anxious as hell. Sinclair was rubbing her palms together and Ardelia had gripped the steering wheel so tightly her palms felt blistery. As they rounded the corner and proceeded down the block, a van pulled up in front of Marge's house. Ardelia continued on past the house, pulling over several houses away. She turned off the car. Sinclair and Ardelia damn near broke their necks trying to see who would get out of the van. A few seconds later, a man and woman got out. As they walked up to the house their identities became visible. Sinclair covered her mouth and Ardelia's fell open.

"That's Thomas and his wife!"

"And isn't that Catherine's car?" Sinclair asked as she gripped a handful of Ardelia's blouse.

Before Ardelia could respond, her cell phone rang. She looked at the number, but it wasn't one she knew. Given all the craziness going on she figured it could be important. Ardelia answered before it went to voice mail.

"Ardelia, I need to see you."

"Cynthia! Oh my goodness, I'm so glad you called. So much is going on and I need to talk to you. Where are you?"

"I know. I know everything. Come downtown. The hotel where I'm staying is directly across the street from the art museum we went to last year."

"I know exactly where it is. What room are you in?"

"410. Hurry up."

"I'll be there shortly."

"That was Cynthia," Ardelia told Sinclair.

"So does this mean I'm not needed any longer?" she asked uncomfortably.

"No girl, you're going with me. Cynthia says that she knows everything that's going on."

"She doesn't know that Thomas, his wife, Catherine and Marge are having a powwow at Marge's house right now. That's hot off the press."

CHAPTER TWENTY-TWO

22

A t the hotel, Cynthia and Leo brainstorm on a strategy

to bring Thomas to his knees. Leo has plenty of money and Cynthia has resorted to her cunning tactics. She put all her bottled up energy to work. Leo was just the connection Cynthia needed to come out of her slump. Leo was the perfect partner since he had residual resentment towards Thomas. Cynthia had come up with a plan that was raw and gritty and she was anxious to execute it. While they plotted, there was a knock at the door.

The moment Cynthia and Ardelia laid eyes on each other, they embraced in a loving hug. Cynthia ushered Ardelia and Sinclair into the room.

"Leo? What are you doing here?"

"Long story, we'll tell you that later," Cynthia answered for Leo.

"Looks like we're in this together after all, huh Leo?"

Ardelia added.

He nodded his head as they all sat at the table to talk. Sinclair
didn't want to feel left out or ignored this time so she stepped up to
give the goods on what they'd seen at Marge's house.

"Oh, hell, no. That bastard is blatantly walking the streets?"
Cynthia said in disbelief.

"Honey, let me break it down even further for you. Marge
and Catherine are sisters and Thomas has a wife!"

"What!? This is making my head spin," Cynthia commented.

"You say they're at Marge's house right now?" Cynthia
asked.

"Yeah," Sinclair replied.

"I'm calling the police and send them over there right now."

"Hold on, flash," Leo said as he took the phone out of her
hand.

"Why?" Cynthia questioned. "He's wanted for several
murders. The police were after him when he got away before."

"I'm not saying don't call, just not at this moment. We need
to get things together here and be able to meet the police at the
house," Leo responded. "Okay, let's hurry up. I want to get all their
asses at once. Thomas has been like toxic waste in my life. We can
get rid of all of them in one fell swoop. Then I can go to the partners
and prove my case. I want my life back and it can't happen to soon,"
Cynthia replied with tears in her eyes.

They put their plan into place and decided to call the police from the car. Leo elected to drive his, black Mercedes E500. As they headed to Marge's house, Cynthia called Detective Emanuel Shelton. She hadn't spoken to him since Thomas left town. Even after all that time, the detective was still smitten with her. Cynthia gave him the highlights since she didn't have time to go into any great detail. This time Detective Shelton reacted immediately. He didn't want to take any chances that Thomas would evade him again. He sent several marked cars to Marge's house.

Detective Shelton wasn't aware that two of his men were closely connected to Thomas, so it was handled as a standard apprehension. Thomas' men overheard the dispatch go out to the police on the street. They called Thomas and gave him a heads up that the police were on their way. Thomas, Janella, Catherine and Marge were already planning to leave, but the call made them move quicker.

In the midst of them preparing to leave, Marge and Janella started to argue.

"Janella, you said there was nothing to connect us to Tony's death. Why did you have to kill him anyway?" Marge yelled.

"He had figured out enough to do us all harm. I wasn't willing to risk it."

"But you were willing to risk another murder on our heads? Your actions have caused me to have to run away from my home. I'm too old for this mess. I only helped because my son needed me and you told me that no one would be hurt. Your word is no good and neither are you. I have only tolerated you for Thomas' sake."

Catherine and Thomas stepped in to control the situation, but it had already gone too far. Marge swelled with anger and Janella wanted to tee off on Marge's ass. Although Thomas loved his mom, if he had to make a choice, Janella would be it.

"Can we deal with this later? We really need to get going," Catherine urged.

"Yeah, let's get outta here," Thomas ordered.

"I don't want to go anywhere with that murderous, slithering cunt," Marge bellowed as she crossed her arms.

"And you don't have to, you old bitch."

Janella's blatant disrespect took Marge by surprise. She slapped Janella across her face so hard Janella staggered.

"Look, we have to go now!" Catherine yelled as she started taking bags to the van.

Mom, Janella, get a grip and grab a bag," Thomas ordered.

Thomas took two bags and followed Catherine to the van. He should not have left them alone. Marge picked up a wire hanger from the sofa and whacked Janella across the back. Janella didn't play fair at all. She retaliated with a shot to Marge's kneecap with her twenty-two caliber pistol.

As Marge fell to the floor, Thomas and Catherine came running into the house.

"What the fuck did you do now, Janella?" Thomas asked sharply.

Janella stood with one hand one her hip, unconcerned by her actions. Thomas kneeled down to check on Marge when his cell phone rang.

"Okay, okay, I'm leaving now. We need an ambulance here," Thomas responded to the person on the other end of the phone. He put his cell phone back into his pocket and told Marge that help was on the way.

"Come on. The police are a few blocks away."

"What about my sister? We can't just leave her here," Catherine whined.

"Then stay and get arrested with her," Janella spewed.

"You're going to be okay Marge, I'll check on you soon," Catherine expressed as she followed Thomas and Janella to the van.

They made it to the corner as the police pulled up in front of the house.

Leo, Cynthia, Ardelia and Sinclair arrived at the same time as the first police car. Two more police cars pulled up shortly after. The officers were given instructions over the radio to wait for the detectives to arrive before moving in. They surrounded the house, waiting for their orders to come.

By the time Detective Shelton and his partner arrived, the uniform officers were ready to kick the door in. Detective Shelton gave the orders, but once the police kicked in the door and they were all inside, Cynthia stood in the middle of the living room floor and screamed to the top of her lungs. They found Marge sprawled in the middle of the living room floor, moaning and groaning in pain, as the blood gushed from her knee. Thomas had gotten away again, but this time he'd left his mother behind seriously wounded.

Cynthia, Ardelia, Sinclair and Leo gave Detective Shelton the whole story, from beginning to end, while the officers combed the house for evidence or leads to indicate where they might be headed. Marge wouldn't reveal anything and pretended to be clueless. Soon thereafter, the ambulance arrived for Marge.

"I guess I'm back to square one. I just can't believe what this man is capable of. I wonder if this is the last time. I hope he's gone forever this time."

"We won't stop looking for him. We'll get him," Detective Shelton said.

"After you've had a chance to review all the evidence, do you think you could meet with the partners at my firm and inform them of what went down? "Sure, but I can't help you get your job back."

"Don't go to them as if you're going on my behalf. It cannot seem as though I'm begging. Just go as if you are following up on some leads in the case. Maybe make mention that Marge has been involved."

"I think I can do it without your coaching," he replied with a big smile.

Leo, Ardelia and Sinclair gathered around Cynthia and walked her out to the car. Leo vowed to keep in touch, and he had given Cynthia enough money to get reestablished. He dropped them off at Ardelia's car. Cynthia asked about Chris and Ardelia told her she had taken her to Lolly's house when things got out of control. She had a burning desire to see her child, so Ardelia took Cynthia straight to Lolly's house.

Cynthia and Chris reunited and Chris went home with them. Since things seemed to have calmed down and Sinclair had lost her husband, Ardelia let Sinclair come home with them. Sinclair was able to make funeral arrangements. They wanted nothing more than to rebuild their lives, so the four of them decided to stay together until they had mended well enough to go it alone.

Slick Thomas, Janella and Catherine were rolling down the highway, feeling pretty good about executing a well laid plan and getting away with it, once again. They were in the wind with no intentions of returning.

The next time you decide to let someone into your life, will you know who you're letting in? . . . Be very careful!!!

-THE END-

Until next time!

Stay tuned for part three;

Compelled: To make the right choice. Coming soon!

To learn more about Shelly L. Foster or share your thoughts visit:

www.ShellyFoster.com

www.royal-peacock-publications.com

rppbooks@sbcglobal.net

Check out chapter one of

Compelled:

To Make the Right Choices

Compelled: To Make the Right Choice

Coming Soon

CHAPTER ONE

1

It's been three years, and several million dollars since

Thomas Alexander wreaked havoc on Cynthia and Chris' lives. During that time Cynthia's has struggled back from the depths of despair. Almost everyone near and dear to her has vanished from her life. Ardelia, her long time friend, couldn't bear the stress and strain of Cynthia's lifestyle so she severed their relationship. Leo, who helped Cynthia with the Savonte', Janella, Catherine and Marge plot, fell by the wayside once he helped finance her road to recovery. Fred, who appeared out of nowhere to help her off the streets, disappeared as quickly as he appeared. Other than her daughter Chris, Cynthia had only one other person in her life. Felicia Dawkins came into her life when she Cynthia a business opportunity that boosted her new architectural firm.

"Thank you for calling the Evans architectural firm. How may I help you?" Chris greeted the caller.

"One moment, please," she replied to the caller.

"Mom, Ms. Dawkins is on line one," she announced to Cynthia on the intercom.

Cynthia chatted with her client and planned a lunch meeting. She hung up and appeared at Chris' desk.

"I'd like for you to join me for lunch. It's time you were more engaged with the clients."

"I'm fine answering the phones. Do I have to?" Chris whined.

"I've been mentoring you for some time and I think this will be a good opportunity. Yes, you have to go."
Chris rolled her eyes and mumbled under her breath as she turned back to her desk to answer the phone.

"Evans Architectural Firm," she answered very nonchalantly.

Cynthia stopped and glared at her for answering the phone like she was irritated that it had rang. Chris placed the call on hold and told Cynthia who was on the line.

"Get your act together and get someone to answer the phones while we're out to lunch," Cynthia snapped, as she went into her office to take the call.

Once again, Chris was rolled her eyes and mumbled. She picked up the phone and dialed the mail room.

"Marge, I need for you to answer the phones during lunch. You'll need to take lunch early so that you can cover the phones while my mom and I take lunch together."

"What time are you planning to leave?" Marge queried.

"'Bout eleven-fifteen."

"I'll be there about five or ten after."

Chris turned her attention back to the paperwork on her desk, shuffling and tossing papers in frustration. Although Chris was ecstatic that she and her mother had repaired their lives, she wasn't interested in being Cynthia's clone.

Cynthia was so busy trying to make up for her mistakes that she didn't give Chris room to breathe. She pressured Chris into working at the firm and now she wanted her equally engaged in the business. Chris agreed to work, but she hadn't signed up for becoming a partner or anything like it. Cynthia constantly put Chris in situations that she couldn't say, 'No' to. If she did, she knew she had to deal with Cynthia's wrath, so she went through the motions.

It was seven minutes after eleven and Marge was approached Chris' desk. Just as Marge reached the desk, Cynthia was coming out of her office. Chris stood, then moved her chair, to accommodate Marge's wheelchair. Marge's kneecap was shattered so badly after Janella shot her that it left her confined to a wheelchair. Not only did Marge feel responsible for Cynthia's hardships, but Cynthia dangled it over her head. To keep Cynthia from pressing criminal charges, Marge agreed to work for her.

When Cynthia was getting her business off the ground, she figured she'd get Marge for cheap and she was right. Marge willingly agreed to work for minimum wage, plus benefits. Of course, Cynthia milked it for all it was worth, working the poor, old woman like a slave. She was used as the office gofer, for whatever needed to be done.

Cynthia nodded toward the elevator and Chris reluctantly followed. They had a quiet drive to the restaurant to meet Felicia Dawkins, since Chris wasn't the least bit interested in meeting this woman, and she sure as hell didn't want to spend her lunch time talking about architecture. Cynthia, on the other hand, had high hopes of grooming Chris to one day take over the business. After Cynthia had literally sunk to her lowest point in life, it was astonishing to see how well things had come together. Cynthia never wanted to relive the traumatic devastation in her life and she'd made tremendous strides in her professional, as well her personal life. She had put all of her energy into starting her business and hadn't given dating a second thought.

By the time they reached the restaurant, Felicia was waiting for them near the front door. Felicia was a petite woman, but she wielded a lot of power for such a small lady. She was sharp and on top of her game. She was well respected and had enough money to do whatever she pleased.

She and Cynthia had a lot in common, since Felicia's husband abused her, too. The difference was that Felicia she walked away from Mr. Quincy Dawkins with a six million dollar settlement. Quincy, who was known about town as 'Q', was filthy rich. Six million dollars didn't put a dent in his pocket. He was a heavy hitter in import and export trade, but had beaten Felicia one time too many. She packed up, took her two children, and left him before she was convicted for murdering his sorry ass.

Another difference between Felicia and Cynthia was that Felicia stayed focused on making a better life for herself and her children. Never once, did she make a decision that caused them harm.

Cynthia and Felicia met by chance and Felicia related to Cynthia's plight. During apple martini's, Felicia agreed to be the Evans Architectural firm's first client. When she signed up, others willingly followed. That relationship was the first brick in building Cynthia's dynamic business. Actually, Felicia used her influence to help Cynthia build her client base. Cynthia's name had been smeared by her ex-partners, but Felicia convinced several of her contacts to give Cynthia a chance. So far, they were all pleased and Cynthia was back on top. Cynthia kept a steadfast relationship with Felicia, and she wanted Chris to develop a relationship with Felicia as well.

As they were seated at their table, Chris' body language was rather melancholy. Cynthia struck up a light conversation to take off some of the strain.

"So Felicia, tell Chris about the concerts you're having at some of your supper clubs."

Chris still wasn't interested, since Felicia and Cynthia's taste in music was worlds apart from what Chris liked. She nibbled on a bread stick until Felicia started to speak.

"We're hosting a tour at three of my locations. I've booked several hip-hop groups...:"

"Hip-hop?" Chris excitedly interrupted.

"Yes. I figured that might interest you. Would you be interested in working with me on the tour?"

Working with Felicia would take Chris away from the firm, and that wasn't quite the relationship Cynthia had in mind for the two of them.

"She has a job," Cynthia interjected.

"This would be on a part time basis in the evening," Felicia replied.

Chris' head moved back and forth, as though she were watching a tennis match, waiting for the next opportunity to chime in, but Felicia and Cynthia didn't let Chris to get a word in edgewise. She grew tired of waiting for an opportunity so she jumped right in.

"I'll do it!" she blurted, as she shifted her eyes in Cynthia's direction. She figured she'd said enough, so she kept quiet for a moment.

Cynthia was a little dewy-eyed, feeling like she'd just lost her best friend. Chris saw the water filling up in Cynthia's eyes and reached over and patted her hand.

"Mom, it's just in the evenings, and only for a few weeks. I'll still be with you during the day."

"But what about when you guys go on the road?"

"It's just a road trip. I'm not moving away."

Cynthia quickly realized how silly she was acting and nodded her approval. Felicia briefly glanced over at Chris and Chris at her then, luckily, the waitress appeared to take their orders.

The brief distraction of ordering their meals was just the break they needed. Although thrilled, Chris contained herself, so Felicia struck up a conversation about work to pull Cynthia back into her comfort zone. By the time their food arrived, the tension had cleared and they were laughing and talking.

Cynthia paid for lunch and suggested that she and Chris head back to the office. Felicia wanted to talk to Chris about the road shows, but thought it best to wait. She winked at Chris as they parted. Chris gave a half-cocked smile in acknowledgement the meaning.

On the way back to the office, Cynthia decided to school Chris on how to handle herself on the road trip. Afterwards, she offered her support. Chris didn't see the need for the speech, but was attentive anyway. She was hyped and anxious about the opportunity, and was so glad now that Cynthia had forced her to go to lunch. Meeting hip-hop stars up close and personal was too good to be true. She planned to stroke Cynthia in any way she had to make it happen. She was going to be the best assistant and the best daughter in the world. She knew Cynthia would need to feel like she wasn't going to lose her child.

When they returned to the office, Marge was holding down the fort as usual. Chris was so pleasant to Marge that she gave Chris a double take. Cynthia went into her office and focused on her work. Marge wheeled down the hallway, glancing back periodically in amazement at how pleasant Chris had been.

The phones were ringing off the hook which grated on Chris' nerves. Her adrenaline was racing with excitement and nothing could bring her down. The next phone call took her even higher.

"Hi Chris, this is Felicia Dawkins' assistant, Ruby Palmer. Can you talk?"

"Yes, yes, of course. What's up?" Chris said enthusiastically.

"I need your e-mail address to send you the tentative schedule of the road shows. Look it over, and Felicia will call you with the specifics."

"Okay, what's the e-mail address you will be sending from?"

"Ruby.Palmer@mail.net. Just look for my name. Call Felicia in a day or so to discuss it, if she hasn't called you."

Chris grinned from ear-to-ear as she hung up the phone. Cynthia stepped out of her office before Chris could erase the smile.

"What's that smile about?"

Chris knew if she told her the truth, her feelings would be hurt again, so she lied.

"That was Lolly telling me about some guy who wants to meet me."

"So, who is he? What's his profession? How old is he?"

"Whoa, hold on, Mom. I haven't met him yet."

Hell, I haven't even had time to conger all that up in my head

yet.

Chris' thought caused her to burst into laughter.

"What's so funny?" Cynthia asked.

"You and all of your questions."

"Shut up, little girl," Cynthia replied as she started laughing, too. She knew how overbearing she could be, and Chris called her on it. She handed Chris some paperwork, then returned to her office. Chris stared at her computer anxiously awaiting the e-mail. She wanted to start planning, but she needed the dates and the.

The day was quickly coming to a close, but the e-mail still hadn't arrived. Chris started preparing to leave for the day and just as she was about to log off of her computer, the e-mail from Ruby Palmer popped into her inbox. She was afraid to show any excitement for fear Cynthia would come out of her office and catch her again, so she kept her cool while opening the message. She hit print then proceeded to log off. As soon as the e-mail printed, she folded the paper and stuffed it into her purse. No sooner than she put the e-mail inside her purse, Cynthia appeared in the doorway. Chris gathered her things and they headed for the elevator.

Chris' cell phone rang as soon as they sat in the car and she was irritated that she hadn't driven to work. She was about to burst with excitement and wanted to share her good news with Lolly, but she had to suppress her enthusiasm until her mother wasn't around.

By the time they made it home, Chris was racing to her bedroom to call Lolly. She finally had enough privacy to look at the printed copy of the e-mail.

"Girl, you will not believe who's performing on this road show!" Chris squealed.

"Who? Who's gonna be there, girl?"

"Eve, Missy and B2K will be in L.A.; the Backstreet Boys, Ninety-Eight Degrees and Black Eyed Peas will be in A.T.L., and girl, the last show is the bomb! Mary J., Snoop Dogg and Beyonce will be right here in Chicago!" she announced, as she bounced up and down on the bed.

"So, can you hook me up?"

"I don't know what I can do yet. Which one do you want to go to?"

"All of 'em."

"All of 'em?! I'm not sure I can make that happen, but I'll try."

"Okay, whatever," Lolly replied, somewhat discouraged.

"Girl, don't sweat it. I got you. Let's go shopping tomorrow."

"Yeah, I can do that. I'll pick you up at your office when I get off work."

"Gotta go, my mom is knocking on my door."

"Yes, Mom? Come on in."

Cynthia poked her head inside the room and asked, "Wanna go get something to eat?"

I'd better suck up or she'll put a cramp in my chance to go on the road trip.

"Sure, Mom. I have a taste for Mexican. What do you want?"

"Mexican's fine. I'm going to change. I'll meet you downstairs in fifteen-minutes."

Almost fifteen-minutes to the second, they were walking out the door.